My hand flew up fro... whether to be a claw or a fist. Wood caught it easily, and applied enough pressure to my wrist to turn coal to diamonds. Smiling, he threw down my arm and advised, "Think about it, Bowering. I have you by the short hairs, and don't you *ever* forget it."

"I believe the lady would prefer that you leave now."

Wood might be pond scum, but not a dummy. He was not about to tangle with a man armed with a sleeping cat. The landlord's eyes did a once-over of Salim, then a longer one of my bare feet and bathrobe.

"Sorry, Bowering, didn't mean to interrupt you while you're 'working.' I'll catch you tonight when you're off duty."

I don't know how the lead crystal candy dish and cover got into my hand. I do know how it shattered against the metal doorframe, spitting M&M's and Hershey Kisses (with almonds) all over the living room. Just call me deadeye.

DORIAN YEAGER

EVICTION BY DEATH

WORLDWIDE.

TORONTO • NEW YORK • LONDON
AMSTERDAM • PARIS • SYDNEY • HAMBURG
STOCKHOLM • ATHENS • TOKYO • MILAN
MADRID • WARSAW • BUDAPEST • AUCKLAND

This book is dedicated to all the people who have
been reduced to working on and behind stage with
me. Especially those who were Auntie "Mame"d.

EVICTION BY DEATH

A Worldwide Mystery/September 1995

First published by St. Martin's Press, Incorporated.

ISBN 0-373-26176-4

ACKNOWLEDGMENTS

For trying to keep me stable: Elyse Thierry,
Immy Bliss, Tom Sinclair, the Abedins, "Broadway
Rose" Sharon Maroney, Big Raymond, Bigger Bill and
those neighbors of mine who were not raised by wolves.
For trying to make me better than I am: C.D.;
Nora Ashoura; my sainted agent, Fran Leibowitz, and
my equally sainted editor, Reagan Arthur; Mitchell &
Associates; Scott Cargle; Barbara Haigh;
Irene Copeland. (See previous book for complete list.)
For giving me a place to eat and hide: the infamous
McAleer's gang and (ringleader) Dee Carmody,
Miss Elle's Homesick Bar & Grill, the Dutch Apple
Theatre, the Limelight Dinner Theatre,
Wandersee Medical Communications.
For those long-suffering souls who have ever been
related to me: in deference to personal privacy—except
Jeremy—I will name no names.

PROLOGUE

NERVOUS BREAKDOWNS are funny things. Despite what my loyal friends contend, *I did not have one*.

I will admit that I went through a period of some agitation, though it was perfectly understandable given the circumstances. Under the circumstances, I think I was a *brick*.

Besides, a true nervous breakdown is generally documented by an extended stay in the Futon Suite at the Hotel Silly, which is not what happened at all. Though it might have been more restful than where I actually landed. I was, admittedly, behaving a bit testily, but then my grandmother always said that I was "highly strung, like a fine racehorse." Bless her heart.

My parents—who never seemed to like me quite as well as dear, darling, Gramma—always claimed I simply had a melodramatic streak. So I guess they ought to be relieved (and it pretty much serves them right) that I ended up becoming a struggling actress with an attitude instead of, say, a gifted nuclear physicist with a flair for the dramatic, wouldn't you agree?

Anyway, I was *not* having a nervous breakdown last fall. A veritable monsoon gale of free-floating anxiety, perhaps, but nothing certifiable. It was just one of those irritating periods when one dippy little thing after another—like the divorce I wasn't so thrilled about getting, my career (ha), my love life (ha, ha), and fundamental domestic security (har-de-har-har)—was out to get me. Is it any wonder that my perfectly acceptable artistic temperament blew like a cheap condom?

Looking back, I guess I just might have been in just the tiniest bit of denial, too. Only a tad. Maybe. Objectively, it is possible that, after having been married for so long, I wasn't entirely... comfortable with having to rely on myself. For everything. Alone.

All right, to be perfectly honest, autonomy... worried me. Slightly. It was a consideration. One might even venture to say that I was fleetingly concerned that, left to my own devices, the probability of my becoming an underachieving bag lady was somewhat better than that of a native Haitian speaking Creole.

In my own defense, being a newly separated thirty-nine-ish woman in New York City is pretty stinko. Being an unemployed actor with no one to fall back on is so mundane as to be boring. But being a love-spurned unemployed actor caught in the middle of multiple homicide is downright, well, murder.

But I think it was not having hot water in my apartment that put me over the edge. They say it's the little things that do it, and a year of cold showers, shampoos, and greasy dishes is a very small thing. At least when compared with bubonic plague. Or world hunger. Or, I don't know, pick one.

Who wouldn't go a little bit nuts?

Besides, as a wise person once said, "Just because you're paranoid doesn't mean they're not out to get you."

I think it was Gramma.

And *nobody* messed with her.

ONE

BODY BAGS are not the best way to start the week, particularly when one is high-strung. They look innocuous enough, but the vision of the slick black polyethylene has an irritating way of slithering into even the most erotic Sean Connery dreams—although things were already going badly enough for me that I'd even started cursing the infrequency of sex during REM sleep.

I was awakened from a sound—and Sean Conneryless—sleep when I heard my upstairs neighbor's body hit the floor or, if you prefer, my ceiling, at about six o'clock in the morning. I recognized the sound immediately since it was far from the first time I'd heard it. Mr. Hillerman had been using a walker for two decades or more, but had never quite gotten the hang of it. This dexterity difficulty caused me to find myself in the back of an ambulance tearing up Broadway to Saint Whoever Hospital approximately once a month, holding Mr. Hillerman's hand and reeling off his vitals by rote to a never-ending variety of EMS paramedics. This being New York City and all, I was always the only boob willing to sign my name to Mr. Hillerman's admittance form.

Being somewhat anal compulsive by nature, I had the drill knocked down to a fine science.

Wearing nothing but my pink cotton nightshirt and a pair of pants, I dragged myself out of my apartment and down the hall to ring Carlotta, the superintendent of the building, to let us in and dial 911. She had been up for hours slamming trash can lids and generally being more efficient than is biologically natural at that hour of the morning. Personally, I am incapable of human speech before eight cups of coffee, so I simply pointed upstairs. Carlotta grabbed her prodigious ring of keys and led the way upstairs.

As always, our knocks on Mr. Hillerman's door went unanswered, so Carlotta miraculously located his key from among the hundreds dangling from the aluminum ring and let us in.

Mr. Hillerman's apartment was unremarkable, except for the teetering piles of ancient newspapers leaning inward from every corner. Since it was directly above my apartment, the floor plan was identical. Owing to the clutter, it appeared half the size.

"Mr. Hillerman?" I called, surprised by my ability to form two words in a row before daylight. A nasty feeling crawled up my back during the ensuing silence. Carlotta waited patiently by the living room door. After so many rehearsals, we had our parts down pat, and mine was to search and find. This time, though, I grabbed Carlotta's calloused hands and dragged her along with me into the kitchen.

Blame my Scottish grandfather or the red hair, but somehow I have the talent to experience ugly stuff twice as often as most other people. While it happens, and before. As gifts go, I'd prefer flowers or chocolate.

As expected, there were no bouquets or bonbons around the corner. We discovered Mr. Hillerman sprawled lifelessly with one-half of an oozing jelly doughnut dangling from the corner of his gaping mouth. I watched the spreading red goo with sick fascination. It was oddly disorienting for me to see normally inanimate strawberry preserves waltzing around the stock-still form of a normally somewhat animate person.

Carlotta sighed and shook her head. As "keeper of the keys," finding deceased tenants was an unavoidable part of her job: one she'd been addressing far too often recently.

Granted, Mr. Hillerman was in his eighties and had been failing for some time, but he was the first natural-death corpse I'd ever stumbled across, and it pretty much threw me off my stride for the day. And night.

And the next night.

I was guilty as sin. You see, a very big part of me was glad to be rid of Mr. Hillerman. Somehow, during the final throes of senile dementia, the old man had decided that I was his older sister, Emily. Somewhere between three and a million times a day, Mr. Hillerman would struggle down the hall stairs and arrive at my door with a shopping list. Often it was precisely the same list he'd given me an hour before, but that never stopped me from dragging myself out to the Korean market on Amsterdam Avenue to buy the identical articles I'd gotten every day for months and schlepping them upstairs for delivery.

Am I a good person? No. Am I a victim of my upbringing? You betcha. Are my good deeds done with a singing heart? Hardly. I called my grocery treks the "grudge trudge." I never said no, but sometimes I turned off the television and pretended I wasn't home. Recognizing what a selfish crud I was didn't do a thing for my self-esteem.

So Mr. Hillerman's apparently natural demise was unfortunate as well as completely demoralizing. Accidental or violent deaths are disorienting, too, I know. But in New York, given credibility via statistics, they're somehow less surprising.

Carlotta interrupted my guiltathon with, "Chu kullde puleetz. Dos yutzes too stupido fur inglis." That is New York/Romanian for "You call the police. Those *yutzes* are too stupid for English." Carlotta's Yiddish, for some unknown reason, is perfectly unaccented. She continued, "I kull de schmuck," meaning she would inform the landlord so he could get the apartment retenanted by the time the coroner's office got the still-warm corpse out the door.

As nearly everyone knows, New Yorkers assiduously scan the obituary column in the *Times* to get early leads on available rent-stabilized apartments. What I knew is that by the time the death notice is published, it's already too late. That's the *true* rationale for keeping superintendents on staff: payoffs. God knows, it's not to do repairs or maintenance.

I located the old black rotary-dial phone under a moldering stack of *Life* magazines from the 1950s. Mildew coated my hands like gloves, and the heavy musty smell made me sneeze as I spoke to the operator to get the number of the Twentieth Precinct. I dialed as I carried the phone back toward the kitchen door, then gave our location and "the problem" to the desk sergeant. Mr. Hillerman's cheek was now lying in a viscous puddle of crimson jelly. The old man had about driven me around the bend, but the indignity of his position made me unutterably sad.

There ought to be a tidier way to die. There's not, of course.

Carlotta caught me before I could wipe Mr. Hillerman's face of the offensive jam with a dishrag. "Nah-huh," she warned. I almost sucked strawberry from my finger before I realized what I was doing. "Lif lon." She was right, of course, so I left it alone and waited with her in the living room for the nearly two hours it took for the authorities to arrive.

"Cardiac arrest," the paramedic pronounced.

"His heart stopped," I translated for Carlotta, who looked at me as though half of my brain had been surgically removed. Of *course* his heart stopped. *Everyone's* heart stops when they die. If the heart were still beating, he wouldn't be *dead*. I knew that. "Yes," I persevered to the white uniform with the bored look, "but do we know why?"

"Shit, lady. This stiff is older than dirt. I don't know why." A flash of minor concern furrowed the woman's brow. "You a relative?" I shook my head no. With the assistance of a burlier paramedic, she closed the body bag over Mr. Hillerman's face with a distressingly final ZZZZZLP. "Then what the hell difference does it make now?" Her assistant looked up at me for the first time.

"Hey," he said, "you're Rick, right?"

"Vic," I amended.

"Right. I was on a call here about two months ago, right?" I examined his face: pleasant, Hispanic, mustache. I didn't know him from Adam, and nodded recognition because it was expected. "I'm Rico, remember?" I nodded again. No reason to be rude. "You were pretty pissed last time about making the trip to ER, huh?"

Okay, so I had an appointment. I was a tad inconvenienced. Okay. It was a lunch date. My almost-ex-husband was buying. So, okay. I was pissed, but I didn't think it showed—let alone that it showed enough to be memorable.

Rico heaved up his end of the body bag with a small grunt. "Well, you don't hafta come along for the ride this time. Life's gonna be easier for you now,

huh?'' The female paramedic shot me a disgusted
look before muscling her part of the load.

"Put it back in your pants, and let's get the hell
out of here, Rico," she grumbled, elbowing past me
in the narrow space. "We're backed up already."

"See ya," Rico said to me on his way out.

I hoped not.

Carlotta's mostly invisible husband, Carlo (I'm
not making this up), appeared in the doorway to an-
nounce that several of my neighbors who lan-
guished in claustrophobic studio apartments had
noticed the EMS van and had started a sign-up sheet
to take a look at the recently vacated two-bedroom
apartment. Carlo figured Carlotta could just stay
where she was and he could start sending them up.

I figured I was fearful of barfing right there on a
mess of old newspapers, so I went back downstairs.

The rest of the day and evening was spent listening to the pounding of hopeful feet up the creaking
staircase, and shuffling over my head. Closet doors
smacked as the upwardly mobile checked out Mr.
Hillerman's storage space. One of my nuttier neighbors from the building next door got into a shriek-
ing match with Carlotta over how long she'd been on
the list for a bigger place and how she was going to
call the housing authority. I chalked all of this chaos
up as justifiable punishment for feeling any sort of

freedom from Mr. Hillerman's hospitalizations and shopping.

At least Mr. Hillerman had not passed unnoticed.

The older I get, the more I realize that going unnoticed is not always such a bad thing.

TWO

ON MONDAY, the construction crew had moved into the vacated apartment—table saws, 87,000-pound work boots, and hammers—to renovate for a quick rental turnaround. In accordance with the rules of work squads worldwide, demolition began promptly at seven o'clock in the morning in the precise spot judged to be nearest my sleeping person. Plaster and grime rained down next to my bed from the opening in my bedroom ceiling through which the hot-water pipe was threaded. I rolled over for some additional shut-eye but couldn't seem to ignore the dulcet "HEY, JULIO, WHAT DA FUCK AM I SUPPOSED TA DO WIF DIS"'s assaulting my eardrums as though transmitted through the gritty pillow next to me. Acoustics are fascinating, don't you think?

Again, irritation at a dead old man reared its ugly head, making me feel guilty anew. It's true I'd been in a monumentally foul mood for about two months, a difficult emotion to sustain for sixty days, I don't mind telling you. At first I had hoped the frazzled disposition and unruly hair was just PMS, but after two full cycles it was apparent even to me that some of that time I had to have been M, thereby negating the P and S parts and that whole hormone rationale.

Responsibility to dead neighbors notwithstanding, it occurred to me that maybe I was having some sort of logical reaction to being unemployed again, but after fifteen years as an actress I should have been adjusted to that annoying poverty stuff. Mere lack of employment ought not to have much impact on a woman who has trained herself as an economy measure never to use more than six sheets of toilet tissue at a time. I was picking up scattered work telling fortunes at the parties of the rich and wannabe famous, which only made me more sensitive to my own pathetic surroundings—but at least it stalled the necessity of cutting down to four sheets of toilet paper. Still, absolutely everything was irritating me, especially callbacks on mornings when I had to shampoo the upstairs apartment out of my hair before even having coffee. Lucky me; I had a callback.

A callback! Another chance for a bunch of producers and a director who'd already seen me strut my audition stuff to take one more uninterested glance at my "party piece." That's like the dumb things your mother used to make you do in front of company to prove that the money spent on lessons wasn't a total waste. What real people would call a monologue. What Navy guys refer to as a dog and pony show. It was not the thrill of my week. It was my third, and it was only Tuesday.

Everyone auditioning actors in New York seemed to be calling me back for another look. Granted, this particular rerun was another shot at the international tour of *Auntie Mame*, and a step up the ladder from the three Polident "go-sees" which resulted in nothing more than a recommendation that I have my teeth capped. But it was still two more subway tokens down the bottomless slot of rejection, and I hadn't even had the foresight to ask for alimony from Barry to help cover such life-rebuilding expenses.

The lukewarm bathwater every morning for the past year wasn't doing anything to buoy my disposition, either.

Did I mention my third annual thirty-ninth birthday was coming up eight days later? On Halloween? Perfect.

Marveling at the deterioration I believed with all my heart had befallen my previously well-preserved body during the night, I dressed in the same boring outfit I'd worn to the initial audition call—which all theater folk will tell you is *very* important, so that the producers (the oppressive slime) can hook on to some clue as to why they called you back.

I tried to keep cat hairs from wafting directly from my feline buddy Slasher's body to the irresistibly magnetic surface of my black spandex dance pants. This farce is, of course, a scientific impossibility, as every woman knows. Having experienced this amusing conundrum approximately three kazillion times before, I threw a roll of pet owners' salvation—masking tape—into my dance bag before leaving Slasher to his breakfast of congealed tuna glop. The light fixtures in my ceilings danced a merry tango to the accompaniment of the demolition of the bathroom above.

The fluorescent halo light outside my apartment door flickered spastically in the long dark entryway. The weary illumination had been fading for so long, I hardly noticed it enough to become further enraged. Shouts for the elusive Julio bade me goodbye.

In the bright sunlight outside the building's entrance foyer, I got my first good look at the ensemble that had become my fur leotard. Carlotta, standing guard over the six adjoining tenements for which she was responsible, was sitting on the stoop as the door slammed caustically behind me.

"Chu godda slatcher onchu," Carlotta offered, meaning "You got Slasher on you," in Carlotta-speak, which I translated unconsciously—the best way, given my rotten attitude. As always, she had cut to the meat of the problem.

"No hot water again, Carlotta," I snapped, trying with some success not to hold her personally responsible. I busied myself in locating the masking tape, making a circle strip of it, and attempting to get the sticky side to pick the cat hair off my clothes. Animal fur is a wonderful substance which, while not actually alive, can manage to weave itself inextricably into any known natural or unnatural fiber. Truly amazing.

Carlotta merely shrugged off the hot-water problem, clearly indicating—as always—that there was certainly nothing she could do about it. She did, however, take the masking tape to my backside. After her efficient ministrations, I no longer looked as though I were wearing Harris Tweed rehearsal togs. I didn't bother to ask how long the international troupe of hard hats would be trying to tunnel through the upper floor down into my place. I'd been through it with the apartment in front of mine the month before and didn't want to know. The black eyes of Mr. Hillerman's windows glared at me unblinkingly. A nasty shudder crawled down the curve of my back.

My usually-best-friend-in-the-world, Fran, appeared from the door of the building two doors east of mine and waved. She looked especially good that morning. I, naturally, hated her for it. Normally, I wouldn't have paid much attention—there's nothing *weird* about our friendship—but we were both headed the same direction, to the same callback, for the same role: Auntie Mame. Neurotic actor-things started running through my mind:

Fran is a brunette; I'm a redhead. Mame is almost always a brunette.

Fran is five-foot-six; I'm five-foot nine. Mame is almost always human-sized.

Fran had dressed better than me for the first audition and, so, was dressed better than me for the callback.

I smiled, wishing she were in South Africa for the touring season, and waved back at her. She gestured for me to wait while she crushed two D'Agostino's grocery bags filled with trash (better trash than *mine*, no doubt) into the large gray plastic sidewalk cans oozing the heavy scent of decomposition outside the door.

I reminded myself that I could not possibly be premenstrual, which was a good thing. A *fine* thing, because if I were going to have a nervous breakdown, I wanted one unadulterated by medical side issues. I wanted my ex, Barry Laskin, to know—deep down in his heart—that it was ALL HIS FAULT. The palpable sensation of Mr. Hillerman's dark apartment accusing me of negligence stabbed at my turned back.

Through the miracle of blame radar, my new landlord, Harvey Wood, slithered out from the front door of the building between Fran's and mine. The mid-October sun made him squint in my direction. Usually he—all polyester shirts and three-hundred-dollar Bally pumps—squints at me for reasons I have yet to fathom. It is never pretty. Much as I was spoiling for a fight, I hoped he was temporarily blinded and would mistake me for an overgrown Irish setter or something. But it was obviously going to be one of those days.

"Victoria, right?" he grunted as he approached. Carlotta heaved herself off the stairs and disappeared into the building.

"Ms. Bowering," I corrected, knowing that decent manners would give him worms. "Harvey, right?" I didn't add, "Like Jimmy Stewart's invisible rabbit, only uglier."

Wood ignored me and further grunted. "Rent-stabilized apartment E?" I ignored him *better*, checked my watch, and looked over his bald head to see if anything besides good sense was holding up Fran. Mr. Synthetic Fabric angled himself in the center of the tenement steps, directly in front of me, before speaking again. "You're the one giving me the pain in the ass with the tenants' association, right?"

"I would expect," I answered, warming up the Rosalind Russell character I was going to need later anyway, "that ass pain—to most men—would be more memorable." I wished I were wearing a fur stole so I could flip an end over my shoulder with a sophisticated flourish. Two white-dusted workmen elbowed past me carrying a plastic trash can filled with wood lath and McDonald's cups. They heaved the whole mess into a dumpster that was slammed up against the scraped bark of the new tree planted in the sidewalk.

Wood knew damned well I was president of the tenants' association. What he didn't know was that I'd been drafted, kicking and screaming, into the position. Unfortunately, as the almost-ex-wife of an attorney, and as a native New Hampshireman—that is, a woman naively convinced of the right to equal application of the law—I seem doomed to spend my life standing on principle and doing Manhattan jury duty.

I looked down and noticed a full white handprint on my thigh. Thanks, Julio.

Fran finally chose to wander over and gesture silently toward the subway we were supposed to be riding at that very moment. Wood looked as though he were weighing the gratification of belting me one in the mouth versus valuable time wasted embroiled in a niggling personal lawsuit. I—being on the verge of a nervous breakdown and all—stepped down onto the sidewalk beside him. Wood twisted at the gaudy onyx pinkie ring on his left hand. No doubt about it, the man wanted to flatten me, big time. He grabbed one of the workmen and told him to have the guys work overtime, he didn't care if it ran twenty-four hours a day, just get it done before the first of the month. He had five stewardesses all ready to move in.

FIVE? My righteous indignation rose right along with the arch in my eyebrow, unconscious and annoying as hell to those on the receiving end. STEWARDESSES? At those times, my common sense and survival instinct go on vacation to faraway lands like Fiji and I become a lean, mean, castrating machine. Temporarily, anyway. Afterward, I always feel as if I'm going to barf.

Fran forgot herself and protested, "Mr. Wood, I called for a bigger apartment *months* ago. I haven't even had a chance to *look* at Mr. Hillerman's."

"Sorry, honey," Wood said to Fran, never taking his eyes off me, "your apartment was renovated last year. Why would I move *you?* Your rent's already up. I move the tits and ass out of their one-bedroom, renovate that, and I get double duty for my time and trouble."

Fran was strangling down a sputter. I'd rather choke to death on a good piece of steak, myself. But Wood was doing one hell of a masterful intimidation job, leaving me stuck—along with my principle—like a brain-dead mastodon in a tar pit of outrage. Under normal, more practical than feisty, circumstances (mine), Wood's tactics to wear me and my best friend down might just have worked, but I had a bed full of ceiling at that moment, so he just pissed me off more than I already was. At least I had Wood to serve as a focal point for my murderous rage. I lit a cigarette.

"A little friendly advice, Victoria," he said back to me, edging closer to my face. "Back off. I'm sick of dicking around with you."

I was dimly aware of a carotid pulse playing reggae in my neck. "I don't dick around with unarmed men," I whispered sweetly, leaning in to kissing distance.

Utterly suicidal, I know. No producer in the world would hire an Auntie Mame who was wearing her aristocratic nose in her hairline.

Wood's face turned the shade of crimson that is a classic symptom of impending myocardial infarction. I took a languid drag off my cigarette, welcoming the possibility of witnessing his blood pump seize up on him in my presence, so crazed with the smell of first blood that I could only smile seductively and blow smoke directly up his hairy nostrils. I felt Fran tugging at my dance bag. I shrugged her off.

"Those MCIs are going through, no matter how you challenge them, Missy," Wood blustered, pulling back out of murderous secondhand smoke distance. "Get it through that red head! Nobody has a God-given right to live in my buildings, and if you don't believe it, ask your friend LaFleur, next door."

I once again crooked my elbow with aggressive condescension, pushing him tantalizingly near the point of outright apoplexy. I suppose, rather than give me the satisfaction of watching him croak like a beached codfish right there on the street, Wood stormed west toward Broadway. Over his shoulder he shouted, "Enjoy your new neighbors, Bowering. *All* of them."

I glared at his retreating back, trembling, on the off-chance he would glance back. He was too chicken, the crud.

"Are you *crazy?*" Fran asked me.

"Let's go," I said, not deigning to answer any query to which the response so obviously had to be YES, I'M CRAZY. That was my landlord I just de-balled. My NEW YORK landlord. My landlord in a city with a 1 percent vacancy rate—and the only reason there are *that* many apartments available is because they don't have WALLS. Or FLOORS. Oh, God.

Hustling off toward the Seventy-ninth Street, Number One subway station, Fran asked, "What MCIs? Didn't we just have another batch go through?"

Ah yes, what about them? MCIs, for those lucky enough not to live in New York City, are Major Capital Improvements. These are "improvements" that landlords make, such as ripping out ornamental oak doors and replacing them with the sort of barricades common in high-security men's prisons, or whacking off the Della Robbia plasterwork on the front of a prewar building and having the facade reworked by Garden State Stucco and Brickface—making the structure eerily resemble alleged mob-boss John Gotti's social club in Queens. Minus the great security, naturally; that would cost extra.

Why? Because New York City says that such "improvement" costs can then be passed on to the tenants, and that all future rent increases will be calculated based upon the higher rent. In perpetuity.

Who says municipal governments have no sense of humor?

"Is Jewel going to be all right?" Fran persisted.

As for Jewel LaFleur, she is the seventy-something housebound ex-stripper I consider the sanest woman I know. She has talked me through every mess I've gotten myself into for the past ten years and has done so with intelligence and a seemingly bottomless stash of good champagne. Those who know me realize what a chore that can be. If I weren't en route to another exercise in futility, I probably would have been sitting with Jewel that very moment, getting advice on how to retaliate for Julio.

Wood had been trying to get Jewel evicted from her floor-through rent-controlled apartment for over a year, ever since he'd bought the six side-by-side buildings on the block. He'd been unsuccessful, but, then, he hadn't been trying all that hard. Now he had motivation: me and my inspirational mouth.

With that nasty light dawning, my righteous indignation thing wore off and the want-to-barf thing kicked in. I didn't dare open my mouth to speak, but since I didn't have any answers for Fran, it didn't matter much. Mostly, I just wanted to get away from the horrific smell of impending doom that permeated my apartment building. Which would have been easier had I been living in America instead of Manhattan.

OCTOBER IS PROBABLY the least disgusting month of the year to be trapped on the New York City subway system. The cars only feel like they're filled with the air from a communal bathroom in a cheap fraternity house about half the time, and the preponderance of the certifiably dangerous vagrant population has not yet moved into the labyrinth of underground cells and tunnels.

Most well-educated people understand the concept of heavy water, but to understand ''heavy air'' you have to ride the IRT. Our local train, the Number One, mysteriously became an express after Seventy-second Street to the accompaniment of much loudspeaker *sturm und drang* instructing everyone to ''Xhfehtgh nem efyuo faorjhjwpgnm oldkjtaeop!''

Newcomers to the city as well as hapless tourists got that glazed look of panic people get when they're trying to look terribly cool but are sickeningly certain their lives are about to come to an ignominious end. We all sailed past the Sixty-sixth Street/Lincoln Center stop. When we didn't even slow down past the Fifty-ninth Street/Columbus Circle station, Fran and I were encased in a horde of terrified commuting victims scrambling to decipher the minuscule subway systems map mounted on the wall behind us. Even if the Transit Authority poster hadn't been smeared over with such aerosol witticisms as BOBO 109 and YO! KISS MY ASS!, all they would have seen would have been a painstakingly illustrated maze of lines in rainbow colors beautifully approximating a schematic diagram of the working components of the space shuttle. Fran and I got up and elbowed our way to the express-side doors.

We were squeezed out of the one operational exit door like pus from a pimple at the Forty-second Street/Times Square stop.

Rather than meander casually through the nude-dance parlors, XXX-rated movie theaters, and sundry other entrepreneurial activities on Forty-second Street proper, we bustled our way through the renowned Metropolitan Port Authority Bus Terminal, and surfaced at Ninth Avenue.

Since the most important thing to remember in this hub of contemporary transportation is to keep your eyes straight ahead, hold on to your purse even though your cash is in your shoe, and look as much like an undercover cop as you can manage, Fran and I didn't break character to speak until we were back above ground on the sidewalk.

"I saw the workmen at your building, Vic. Have they started on Mr. Hillerman's already? Damn, but I wanted that extra room. I've been trying to get a repair on a broken pipe in my bathroom for three months. Can't even get that."

"They invaded at seven A.M. If this lasts more than a week, I swear I'm going to take a nail gun to the entire crew. Julio, first."

"I wondered where Julio went. They've been working on the Rivera apartment for weeks now in my building. After the accident, the whole family upped and moved back to Puerto Rico. Gives me the shivers just thinking about it."

Mrs. Rivera had been plowed down and killed by a gypsy cab crossing Broadway, right in front of Zabar's Deli, not a block away from home. No identification, no prosecution. I love New York, indeed. Fran went on.

"Wood had the renovators in before the toilet stopped flushing."

I'd forgotten the Riveras. The dumpsters had been parked on the block for so long, I'd stopped noticing them. The family had lived in one of the last remaining floor-through apartments. Wood had the front-to-back area hacked up into one-bedroom and two studios faster than you could say, "Look both ways before crossing the street."

"How many apartments are vacant in your building now, Fran?"

"Three. No, two. Wood rented the Silvermans' to a Peruvian folk band."

"You're making that up."

"You mean you can't hear them from only two doors down? How many are empty in your building?"

"Just Mr. Hillerman's. Wood's already rented it to the contenders for the Swedish bikini team. Whatever happened to the good old days when there were no more than four to a shower massage? I'm going to get him, Fran, if it takes the rest of the best years of my life to do it."

"Doesn't Wood scare you, Vic?"

"How stupid do I look?" I answered. "He scares the shit out of me. I think he's paying off the city building inspectors. That last MCI went through the system like bad seafood through a French Canadian, even though the work was never done. I got an engineer's report saying so and challenged the increase."

"How did I miss that?"

"You were doing that cruise ship gig. Anyway, the inspector came back to pay me the courtesy of telling me in person that I was obviously mistaken, and now we're going to be paying for something we never got for as long as we live in the buildings. Wood's been trying to evict me from the moment he laid eyes on me. If my ex didn't represent me in housing court for free, I'd have been on my butt months ago. I don't know what to tell Jewel. Marry an attorney?"

"Wood's been all over you like white on rice because he wants to boink you," Fran offered sagely.

"Excuse me? Literally or figuratively?"

"Oh, get off it, Vic," Fran grumped, stepping over a chestnut-bearded man who had apparently fallen victim to a nap attack and was weathering it out in a prone position over a storm grate. "You'd think the man had never seen a thirty-three-inch inseam before. I hate it when you pretend not to notice men sexually harassing you."

"I didn't notice it was sexual," I protested innocently. Besides, my inseam measurement is thirty-five inches, not that I'm *vain* about it. "I thought it was personal. Wood treats me like something you scrape off your shoe.''

"You're a woman," Fran said over her shoulder as she turned north on Tenth Avenue. "This is New York. Wake up and smell the coffee.''

I grimly accepted the truthful implication of that statement while we walked two blocks up to the rehearsal studio.

You see, in New York City, single, straight, over-thirty males are outnumbered by single, straight females by approximately 47,854 to 1. A hunch-backed male dwarf with the thinnest veneer of heterosexuality and the IQ of plankton has a better than decent chance of getting lucky with a professional runway model in Metropolis. I have no idea why this bizarre incongruity of the natural order of the species seems to make Manhattan men so testy. I suppose, because they're allowed.

"All I know," Fran said, "is that I would never have gone into this association business with you if I'd known what kind of turnover we were going to start having in the buildings. Every time someone dies or moves out, the tenants get weaker. Illegal aliens and *ménages à cinq* don't like to rock the boat.''

Also true. Of the twenty apartments in my building, only eleven of the original tenants were left. Six had been harassed out by Wood's lawyers; one had not been able to keep up with the three rent increases of the past eight months; and two—like Mr.

Hillerman—had died. However, I don't think I could be held responsible for Fran's inability to reject my begging and pleading. We both attended the same assertiveness seminar the week after Barry walked out on me taking everything that plugged into a wall socket with him.

Fran asked if I was going to do the same monologue I'd done at the first audition for the producers, distracting me from dwelling on Wood's responsibility for the tenancy carousel, and Barry's for my life without a coffee grinder.

I told Fran I thought we were going to be doing cold readings—that is, a reading from the script itself. Holding the pages. A no-brainer. She didn't think so. I was pretty darned sure I couldn't *remember* my monologue. I don't sleep very well alone, so my concentration has been shot since the day my ex-husband, Barry, moved out. That's almost a year of sleep deprivation. I'd forgotten. Almost.

It was emphatically going to be one of those days.

THERE IS SOME KIND of inviolate rule that elevators never arrive in buildings with theatrical rehearsal space, so without even giving it a try, Fran and I sprinted up seven floors. Once there, wheezing provocatively, we surveyed the competition. At one glance we separated the Auntie Mame types from the frumpy Miss Gooches. Dividing Mames from Veras was an impossibility, since the roles are for all intents and purposes interchangeable, so we relied on years of experience and professional behavior.

"How do I look?" I asked, without much optimism, blindly counting on a decade of Fran's friendship for groundless support.

"Your hair's getting really frizzy from sweat," Fran answered reassuringly.

Sure enough, I could feel the little red ringlets crimping up on my forehead—not a bad thing at an *Annie* call, but less than swell for a sophisticated comedy. I felt like Shirley Temple trying to bag a role in *Body Heat*. Hopeless. Depressed. Anxious. I'm sorry, even *more* anxious. I couldn't afford to have a nervous breakdown until I had enough weeks of work logged to qualify for unemployment.

"How do I look?" Fran asked, oblivious to my total collapse of self-esteem.

"Perfect."

I hated her and every other straight-haired brunette in the room. There were fourteen. I counted. I was being sucked into a spiral of masochistic despair. I felt like an . . . actor.

"Okay, people, listen up!" shouted the monitor, that poor boob who was in charge of keeping a roomful of people like me, teetering on the brink of emotional collapse, firmly in hand. He continued confidently—sure, HE had a job—"As you know, this is an international tour. We go into rehearsal in one week." He looked up from his clipboard blandly, "Dancers, that means seven days, November first, in L.A." It's a showbiz rule that everyone, even stage managers, makes fun of dancers. "Anybody who has a problem with that, talk to me at the end." One of the competition fell theatrically into a heap in one corner of the large, airless room to check her appointment book. Fran and I looked at each other with unkind mutual pleasure. "Five-week rehearsal, open for limited preview run in L.A. Fa-la, say goodbye Santa. Then to San Francisco, Chicago for Valentine's, six weeks in Houston, see the Easter Bunny in Boston, and finally every hofbrau in Germany for another eight. We'll bury this sucker in Tokyo if there's any money left. Anyone without a valid passport, see me at the end. Now, we're reading people in groups, so everybody has to stick around. Shouldn't take more than six hours. Anyone with problems, see me at the end. Mames and Veras will be switching off, so Gooches may be reading with the same people several times. Any-questions-good." Wise man that he was, he disappeared.

I almost relaxed. We'd be reading from the script. Cold readings are my favorites, primarily because most actors flub and freeze. Bless the American school system.

"I hate cold readings," Fran sighed and sat on the floor. The monitor reappeared from wherever he'd been hiding from the actors waiting to talk to him and started calling off names. "I need this job. It's going to be a year of work," Fran muttered. "It's a chance to check out L.A., to see something besides the inside of Zabar's cheese department." She stood up, looking ill. "Maybe afford an apartment that's *not* rent-stabilized." She sighed with determination. "I'd better go warm up."

Now, personally, I don't know how to warm up for a non-musical. Even *for* a musical, I usually just step outside and smoke until I hear my name called. No one was even going to be asking to hear me sing, so I pulled a Larry McMurtry novel out of my dance bag and pretended I didn't give a shit if someone else got cast in the role I'd spent my entire life getting old enough to play; that would bail me out of a financial situation that made the Soviet Union or whatever it's called this week look bright; that would bolster my rapidly evaporating self-image, would keep me out of an office job and a suit for yet another year; and—most important—that would requalify me for unemployment. I'm afraid actors are not the best long-term planners in the world.

Fran and I read the audition scene for the producers together four times, switching between the plum lead role of Mame Dennis, and Mame's sidekick, Vera Charles. I found myself flipping character analyses between a derivative Bea Arthur and a demented flamingo. Both choices involved lots of flapping arms and slow takes. I scared myself. After three hours or so, I couldn't imagine feeling worse.

In my business, I should have more imagination.

We were all dismissed without a clue to our futures. I took this to be a good indication, always preferring to get my rejection behind my back where I could more efficiently ignore it.

"So," Fran shouted over the clatter of the subway on the trip back to the Upper West Side, "how are you going to handle the forest troll tomorrow night?" I shook my head to indicate total lack of comprehension. "Wood," Fran screamed into my good ear, "at the tenants' meeting. What are you going to do for Jewel? She depends on you, you know."

I knew. It demoralized me sufficiently that I gave a quarter to the first three panhandlers who asked, even though they weren't "my" beggars. Being guilt-ridden by virtue of genetic composition and up-bringing, I've chosen two neighborhood beggars to whom I always give money. That way I only feel kind of rotten when I refuse the other forty-or-so requests I get a day. Of course, the seventy-five cents I handed out was all I had left in my wallet.

I most definitely felt worse all the way home.

I didn't know what I was going to do. About any-thing. What good *is* a demented flamingo, anyway? They don't even make decent lawn ornaments any-more.

I thought I needed a change. I thought I needed something to occupy my mind now that Mr. Hillerman had been dispatched to that great Korean grocery in the sky.

When am I going to learn to stop thinking?

THREE

Later

SOMETHING WAS WRONG with my apartment. I had a creepy feeling from the moment I opened the door—a different creepy feeling from the one I had when I left—and my creepy feelings are never completely unfounded. It's a gift. Not as good as jewelry, but still, a gift.

The metal door rattled shut behind me as I surveyed the space. The walls needed painting, of course. They had for some time. Too bad slimeball landlord Wood only bought institutional tan in economical oil drums for the purpose of freshening his tenants' homes. So that wasn't what was niggling at me. A tremendous crack had appeared down the center of the living room ceiling from the attack of the killer construction workers upstairs. All easily explainable. Still, the hair on the back of my neck stood up with better posture than normal.

My attack cat, Slasher, opened one eye and fell back into a deep, snoring sleep. I was not reassured by his lassitude. Slasher could nap through a championship Lambada competition. Proving it, he didn't budge through an especially chilling screech for Julio's assistance, followed by the crash of what must have been Mr. Hillerman's toilet bowl. I dropped my dance bag and peered into the dim recesses of my north-facing first-floor railroad flat. Everything seemed all right. Black as the inside of a cow's gut, but in order. Sure, you slimebucket landlord, I cursed Wood, paint old Bossie's insides TAN. That's a real mood elevator.

The kitchen faucet was running a thin stream. Turning it off, I noted that the water still wasn't hot. I flicked on the light in the bathroom and checked behind the shower curtain— très *Psycho;* no Janet Leigh droppings there.

A dull glow of light wept in through the bedroom window. I had to kneel on the bed to test the super-duper NYPD-approved security gate, and stick my nose through the metal lattice to search for any sign of intruders on the fire escape or in the back alley "garden." Nothing. Nonetheless, my nerves were jangling like a cheap fire detector.

Feeble as the light was, I could make out the snowy white of Slasher-fur upholstering the knees of my black leggings, so I wandered back toward the kitchen for another application of masking tape, cursing Barry for giving me kitty custody. The wall shuddered violently, sending my copper mixing bowls into a clattering convulsion.

Then it hit me.

Someone had been in the apartment while I was gone.

You see, there are two things that make me crazy—
sorry, more crazy than previously documented—
wasting paper and wasting water. I would no more
have left my house with a faucet running than I'd
throw out a piece of scrap paper with more than an
unused square inch. Sure enough, there was a dino-
saur-bedecked jelly glass upside down in the dish
drainer, still speckled with water drops. Not mine. I
use one coffee cup a day, generally my Di and
Charles royal wedding commemorative, period, for
coffee, water, milk, juice, bourbon. My mother
swears that someday it'll kill me: all those germs
backed up and waiting to attack my delicate internal
organs.

It had taken a while, but she was right. A germ had
finally been visited upon me.

Obviously, I'd had another surprise inspection
visit from the infamous tenement-fairy, Harvey
Wood.

"Damn!" I shouted at the perfectly innocent jelly
glass. Slasher twitched to attention from his favorite
spot on the sofa and eyed me suspiciously before
settling back into cat coma. "Damn!" I elaborated
over the shouts of Julio's coworkers and the crash of
a window being pushed out and down into the air
shaft.

Between worrying about stupid, probably futile
auditions; the upcoming tenants' meeting; my dwin-
dled bank account; impending divorce; third annual
thirty-ninth birthday; overhead gutting by the intel-

lectually challenged; and cat hair ALL OVER EVERY-THING when I hadn't even thought to ask for kitty-support, I became a bit overwrought. Perhaps I overreacted.

I called the cops.

Well, not *the* cops. I called *my* cop, Detective Sergeant Daniel Duchinski, NYPD. Unfortunately for him, his beeper number was on my telephone auto-dial. I'm certain I was too strung out to look any-thing up. I punched the button, and at the tone punched in my own number. Directing select phrases of ancient Anglo-Saxon at Slasher for shedding IN HIS SLEEP, for God's sake, I peeled off my dance pants before moving his slack body to the opposite side of the sofa and thudding down on MY side. I heard a support bar crack beneath me. Perfect.

Duchinski was on my shit-list du jour, too. After a year of seeing each other steadily (between surveil-lances, drug busts, and sundry interdepartmental scandals, natch) our physical relationship was stalled at petting. Yes, the icing on my third annual thirty-ninth birthday cake was that I was dating a man who believed that having sex with a woman who was still legally married to another man was WRONG. I wouldn't lie about a thing like that. It's too bizarre. Most of the men I encounter in the city would hap-pily have sex with a bullet wound, legally separated or not.

All right, in fairness, I guess I wanted to be in love. I guess I needed to. If love is blind, maybe it could render me deaf, as well. Okay, okay, so it was probably already too late for me to fall. I had probably been felled weeks before. But you have to admit, when a *man* says no, it's a bit off-putting to the old fragile feminine ego.

I glared at Slasher. I fixated on the rampant corruption of New York City: the sleeze; the noise—I thought I could make out the vague strains of Peruvian flutes over the demolition din; and most of all, the utter, profound irony of having the kind of shitty karma to get involved with a man with ETHICS, of all things. No wonder everyone was commenting on my instability.

My frog phone burbled, and I suddenly hated my pretension of owning a telephone that masqueraded as something other than a communications device— let alone an amphibian most commonly used as freshwater bait. I picked up anyway after the first BLUB, flipped down the back legs, covered my free ear with my hand, and answered into the green belly.

"Dan."

"Hi, babe, I was just on the..."

"Well, it took..."

"It did not."

"WHAT?" I shouted over the crash of cabinets being ripped from walls.

"I SAID, I did not. What the hell is going on there?"

"Mr. Hillerman died."

"In what? A guerrilla attack?"

"Cardiac arrest. Wood's bozos have already moved into rehab."

Dan paused. "So hit me with it."

"Who said there was a problem?" I answered his question before he asked it, as usual, and lit a cigarette. I missed Dan, despite my mood. The same old same old.

"You did. You only answer the phone with my name when there's a problem. You answer with your name when you're feeling officious. Otherwise, you say hello like a normal person."

Since he was right, I decided not to argue. "Maybe I missed you. Isn't that possible?"

"No," he responded thoughtfully, "*that's* not it."

"Oh, for heaven's sake, no it's not," I grumbled, and launched into a fuming tirade about the violation of my privacy. From there I proceeded into an eloquent diatribe, finishing up with a succinct string of four-letter physical impossibilities.

Dan let me catch my breath. "Snit over?"

"No."

"So," he ignored me, and answered the question *I* hadn't yet asked, "you want to know if it's legal for your landlord to be in your apartment in your absence."

"No." I snitted, knowing from Dan's patient tone that it *was* legal. "I want to know if you'll break the little crud's arms and legs."

"Sorry, Vic, I'm a little backed up right now. But why don't you come downtown and I'll buy you lunch. You can have anything you want as long as it's Indian.''

I was tempted. Actors can rarely resist things like free food. ''Will you hug me, and kiss me, and call me 'Baby'?'' I asked, perversely mellowing, considering I wasn't getting any of the answers I wanted so far. But before I got a friendly, positive noise, I remembered my lunch date with the man who was responsible for my enforced celibacy: my almost-ex-husband, Barry Laskin. Damn. I couldn't figure out a way to get two free lunches. ''Damn!'' I interrupted myself for a change. Above me, it sounded as though Julio and Company had moved in a forklift.

''Never mind,'' Dan said without hearing the phony excuse I was searching for. ''How about dinner tonight?'' Without taking a beat, he continued, ''We'll order in Chinese after I hug you and kiss you and call you 'Baby.' Slasher loves cold sesame noodles.''

What's not to love about a guy like that? I made all the proper appreciative sounds, visions of Dan's great hairy arms wrapped around me, leaning back against his huge—admittedly somewhat overweight, but hard—body, how maybe I could get him a little bit drunk and then take advantage of him when . . .

BLAHHHHHHHHHHHHHHHHHHHHHHT. The door buzzer fired off.

''Sorry, Dan, it's the door.'' BLAHHHHHHHHH-HHHHHHHHHHT. ''That's got to be Barry. See you later.'' I hung up and lunged for the door before the buzzer could screech again. I was on sensory BLAHHHHHHHHHHHHHHHHT overload. Too late. While putting my pants back on, I hit the button on the intercom that releases the lobby door, heard it open, and grabbed my purse. I opened the apartment door at the first rap.

Barry was dressed in lawyer garb, carrying an expensive briefcase; hardly what I expected for a social lunch. He leaned forward to kiss me at the precise moment I released the knob and turned to check that my answering machine was on. Barry managed to block the closing door with his oxblood loafer before it rearranged his boyish face.

"Sorry," I apologized, kissing him on the cheek, smelling his new aftershave. Italian. Expensive. Not the Whatever-My-Mother-Gave-Him-For-Christmas of which I was so fond. "I'm a little scattered today." And every day I see Barry, which is just about every day. Fran says that's neurotic. Jewel says it's masochistic. Go figure.

"Your new door buzzer sounds like an enraged badger."

"How do you know what an enraged badger sounds like?"

"U of Wisconsin law school mascot." There was a thunderous thunk from upstairs that rattled my ceiling fan. Barry jumped. "What the hell?"

"Urban renewal," I explained loudly.

"Oh. Where do you want to eat?"

"The usual is fine. Any shift in the norm could tip me over the edge this afternoon."

"Just this afternoon," Barry tossed off, following me down the institutional tan and institutional brown hallway as we narrowly missed a two-by-four that tumbled down the stairwell.

ONE OF THE nicest things about "the usual," McAleer's Pub, is the fact that it's always, unflaggingly, exactly the same.

Except for that afternoon.

Timmy, my favorite actor/bartender, was not on duty. Neither was Doug, my second-favorite actor/bartender, nor Tom, my third favorite actor/bartender. My delight in being treated to lunch didn't precisely evaporate, but it dissipated a bit. Apparently, it showed on my melodramatic face, because the total STRANGER behind the bar grabbed the remote control and turned down the sound on the television mounted on the brick over the entryway. I was toying with the idea of behaving completely childishly and leaving, when the new guy—the STRANGER—spoke.

"Lost?"

Barry checked his watch, trapping me in the door. I was feeling perfectly unreasonable, prickly with irritation. I didn't like the new bartender's attitude. Lost, indeed. Hell, I didn't like the new total-stranger bartender. What was he doing there instead of

Timmy, or Doug, or Tom? Didn't I have enough upheaval in my life without THIS?

"Can we sit down now?" Barry asked me from behind. It startled me, and interrupted my consternation.

"Sure, what the hell," I muttered, striding toward the bar. I'd show HIM. I wasn't about to let some stranger, some interloper, get in the way of me and a medium-rare cheeseburger with well-done fries. Fuck him if I can't take a joke.

"You're in a mood," Barry offered sagely, plunking his briefcase behind the foot rail. The leather was initialed. Barry hates initials on things. No doubt a gift from whatever tawdry slattern he was dating at the moment—though I'm sure she's a very nice person, inside, where it *really* counts. My brow furrowed, I believe. "Order me a Guinness, I'll be right back."

I watched my almost-ex close the men's room door behind him and turned back to the bar, straight into the face of the carpetbagger/bartender. His eyes were gray as pewter, a smooth match for his soft salt-and-pepper hair. He was leaning forward attentively and smiling a crooked smile. It was lopsided and utterly charming. I hated him for that. I was not about to have my nervous breakdown—excuse me, collapse—invalidated by casual pleasantness. So I attacked shamelessly.

"You don't *look* like an actor," I accused.

"I'm not," he answered, still balanced forward on his crossed arms, a foot away from my petulance. If he ever stood up, he'd be tall, I noticed. Quite tall. Tall enough to waltz with. His smile never wavered, though his forehead crinkled inquisitively.

"What?" I countered cleverly. It's too bad that actors can't afford vacations. I was acutely aware that I looked as though I needed one.

"Can I get you something to drink?"

"Oh." Yet another stellar comeback. "A Guinness and a Rolling Rock, please. Pints."

"No Rolling Rock." He didn't move; I stared dumbly. "No Rolling Rock," he repeated patiently. "Miller Genuine, Miller Light, Guinness, Genesee."

Now, I don't much like beer, but I *always* drink Rolling Rock at McAleer's. I always had lunch at McAleer's with Barry because it was the one place in the world where I wouldn't be called upon to make a decision or meet anyone new. And there were always enough leftovers to take home. Hell, McAleer's was the last bar in America that still had a real cloth towel-on-a-roller machine in the Pepto-Bismol pink ladies' room. It was a refuge, home. Now *this*. I felt tears well up in my eyes. Obviously, I was in worse emotional condition than even Barry could imagine. Rather than give my tormentor the satisfaction, I stifled my traitorous tear ducts and glared back into the gray, gray eyes of the Hun who was maliciously denying me my comfort beverage.

"Interesting," he said, finally standing upright and drawing a pint of Guinness, "your eyes turn green when you cry." He put the glass down in front of Barry's briefcased spot and leaned forward on his arms again into my personal face-space.

"I'm not crying." His forehead recrinkled. "I'll have a Genny, thank you." He swung back, still smiling. I reminded myself that, as a woman on the verge of total nervous "collapse," I didn't need to be polite, or even sane, so I thrust further. "If you're not an actor, what are you doing behind the bar?"

Aha, I got him there.

He set my glass of not-Rolling Rock down and slid a coaster underneath. "I'm a bartender."

Clever. Very clever. Insidious answer.

I realized in a shot why people having total nervous collapses get locked up. We don't make any sense. The bartender lit a cigarette for himself and one for me. I took it in a daze. The worst part of behaving completely irrationally is those transitory spurts when you know you're doing it.

"How did you know I smoke?" I asked, settling down.

He pointed at the large plate-glass window. "I've been watching you walk by for a couple of weeks now. You go to the greengrocer next door and buy kitty litter about every three days. Your name is Vic Bowering and you're an actress." He took a smug drag off his cigarette and grinned. "I asked Timmy.

You also have the longest legs I've ever seen off a
racetrack, which I could see for myself."

I wasn't sure if an animal husbandry comparison
was the sort of comment that requires a thank-you,
so I sipped my beer and concentrated on behaving
like a multiple personality victim.

"You're welcome," he said, making me feel
somehow gauche. The man was impossibly irrever-
ent. "Sorry to hear about old man Hillerman. That
must have been rough, finding him."

"How do you know about that?"

"Bartenders know everything. It's a perk." He
flicked ash from his cigarette onto the floor.
"Frankly, no matter how much Hillerman drove you
crazy, you don't look the type to whack him."

"WHAT?"

"I don't believe everything I hear."

"What did you hear?"

"One of the paramedics that came for Hillerman
thought his death was suspicious. You especially.
Personally, I think she was just jealous of you. She
and Rico have had a thing going for some time, and
everyone knows he's a leg man."

"You know," I stated with composure, "I always
figured that's what you guys do in here all afternoon long: gossip, watch unsuspecting people walk
by, and make snide remarks."

That's right. Just because you're paranoid doesn't
mean they're not out to get you.

"We do it at night, too, if it's not too busy." He stuck out his hand without apology. I shook it, figuring I'd been bourgeois enough for one day. "My name's Ivan Stepanek, and you were right, I'm not a professional bartender. I was an international investment banker until I was laid off a few months ago, so we should have dinner sometime to discuss your intuitiveness. And the evils of *glasnost*. And here comes your date." Ivan gestured with his eyes to Barry, making his way back to his seat at the bar.

"He's not technically my..."

"That's better. It makes me so tense when you get in your moods," Barry stated, sitting down and breaking up what little intrigue I'd managed to muster. Ivan sidled to the opposite end of the bar and turned the volume back up on the television. Oh, well.

"I'd noticed."

"So," Barry asked, "how are things going?"

I turned my attention back to the man to whom I'd been married for ten years, made a few feeble attempts to get further into a sentence than the word "I," and then surrendered to a torrent of quivering lips and not-crying. Apparently it was a quiet enough spasm not to draw attention. Ivan never even turned his head.

Barry walked me back, out of sight, behind a pillar that delineated the dart-throwing area from the heavy drinking area. To his credit, he put his arms around me and let me stutter it most of the way out. His arms felt just right: warm and familiar.

"Vic, what is it? Vic, talk to me."

"Oh, Barry, I don't...know. Nothing. Everything."

We sat at the nearest green-plastic-covered table. The pony-tailed cook came out of the kitchen and plugged a quarter into the pay phone directly behind us. Barry's brown eyes warned me not to project my voice. Barry hates theatrics. Under the conditions, I must say he was behaving admirably— for him.

How could I explain to a man who was in the process of dumping me that I didn't seem to be taking it all very well? I might not have any discretionary income, but I did have my pride.

Whoopee.

Avoiding topics like the fact that I missed him so much sometimes that my skin hurt, I launched into a distillation of superficial personal misery: the flapping flamingo callback that morning, the run-in with my landlord, Harvey Wood; and getting Carlotta to open up Mr. Hillerman's apartment so we could be the first to see him dead—probably of malnutrition or something that I could have prevented, were I a decent human being. Rather than lose my audience, I skipped the Peruvian Lawrence Welk problem down the block. It was with uncharacteristic discretion that I sidestepped my sexual frustration over Dan Duchinski's refusal to have sex with me—especially since my only other regular date, Brad Sinclair, a newsman on one of the local TV stations, had upped and married some other woman. A straight-haired woman, no doubt.

I *did* whine at some length about how when I looked in the mirror lately I was seeing my mother. That topic rapidly deteriorated into a profoundly boring monologue chronicling everything that was horrible about the way I look. I can go on for days with that one. Rather than suffer, I suppose, Barry jumped in.

"Vic, for God's sake, listen to yourself. Now, I have to agree that as far as careers go, well, you don't have one. But the one thing I *do* know is that whenever we walk into a room, every man around about breaks his neck to get another look at you."

"Disbelief," I sulked, not to be placated by sweet talk.

Men just don't get it. Maybe they have different eyeballs than women do. Maybe they're just from a different planet. God knows men—with the exception of David Letterman—never have really bad hair days. I believe Barry jumped back in to prevent me from running down the long list of things I found really disgusting about my appearance.

"Despite your rotten attitude, you might just get that tour job, you know," he said, handing me a handkerchief. "Someone has to get it."

"Sure," I swiped at my nose—the one with the ugly little bulb at the end of it, "as soon as they clear up that peace in the Mideast thing."

"Food's up," Ivan said as he walked past us into the kitchen to get our lunches.

Barry and I went back to the bar like obedient children.

"At least try to do some affirmations," Barry urged. "Or is it that you don't really want the tour?"

"Want doesn't cover it. Emotionally, I just can't afford to want it and then not get it," I griped. "It's too perfect. It would solve all my problems." Not the least of which was being in the same city with Barry when the stupid part of me still wanted him so much. "The money is fabulous. The exposure is better. It could mean the turning point of my career, if you'll pardon my use of the 'C' word."

It would also occupy my mind, keeping it off items like tenants' associations, poverty, and revolving stewardesses who, no doubt, had actual sex lives. Several with Barry, no doubt.

"You should do something to take your mind off it," Barry advised through a mouthful of cheeseburger. Thank you, Ann Landers. "Go out and work in that garden of yours. You love that."

I loved you, too, you bozo.

The garden was a good idea, anyway, not that I would admit it. For three years I'd been working out my frustrations trying to get anything in the world to grow in the back alley. Most plants require at least some indirect sunlight for photosynthesis, so my luck hadn't been the best. The begonias were blooming valiantly, however, and I had the start of a rather impressive moss and fungus display. When I mistakenly believed I couldn't get more miserable in August, I sent a Polaroid of it to the "Victory Garden Amateur Horticulturalist Contest." Public television could use more puckishness, in my opinion.

"Oh, God," Barry said suddenly, "Look at the time." He grabbed his briefcase, threw money down on the bar, and kissed me quickly.

"But what about the tenants' association? I had some questions!"

"No time."

"Barry," I protested, also standing and grabbing my purse.

"Vic, I'm *late*." He headed to the exit; I followed. "Look, Wood can't evict you unless you've broken your lease; you haven't done that, so RELAX, work in the garden. If my, uh, appointment for that night falls through, I'll try to make the meeting."

Appointment, indeed. Every time I thought I'd adjusted to Barry's life without me, the old jealousy monster started munching on my insides.

On the street, I asked, "What about Jewel?"

"Jewel's on her own, I'm afraid. I can't do pro bono work for *everyone* on the Upper West Side, Vic." With that, he hailed a cab and was on his way off to who-knows-where. To who knows whom. I just stood for some minutes, like one of my prize mosses. Ivan tapped on the picture window of McAleer's and waved good-bye. Nothing to do but go dig in the dirt, I supposed.

Maybe eat some worms.

I WAS MILDLY SURPRISED, as always, that Harvey Wood hadn't changed the lock on the door to the basement of my building. My old landlord, Mr. Feldstein, allowed me to enter through the cellar door to get to the back alley and my "garden." It was paved, it was dank, and it was dark, but it was my solace through a lot of bad times—most of them named Barry—and it was mine. I kept raunchy old jeans and sneakers by the back door, along with my horticultural tools so that I didn't trail *too* much grime back into the furnace room or upstairs, into the residential zone.

Just putting on my hobby clothes—albeit in the dark, since the dangling light bulb had been removed—made me feel almost human. I reassured myself that the oppressiveness I felt was due to some primeval fear of total blackness and grabbed a handful of kitty treats for the mob of alley cats whose sole pleasure in life seemed to be ferocious mating in my raised flower beds. My loose plan was to get started with sweeping up whatever rubble had been thrown from Mr. Hillerman's windows. I'd been through the same thing with old Mrs. Pearlman's rehab and was prepared for the worst.

The reminder of the two old people bumped clumsily against the still untamed jealousy monster in my gut, making me fleetingly queasy. Five long, deep breaths quelled the low-grade nausea, if not the kinetic unease. My blood pressure was negligible as I groped down the length of the door to locate the knob and push my way outside. The rusty hinges squealed in protest. In disbelief, I dropped the cat munchies where I stood in the door; herds of mangy felines darted in about my feet to snatch nuggets of kibble.

My eyes strained painfully to adjust to daylight, my mouth flopped unattractively open, and my blood pressure surged like floodwater against sandbags.

The garden looked like bad press for the South Bronx: gutted, flattened.

The bricks that held back the hundreds of pounds of soil—bought, for MONEY, in New Jersey of all places—had been kicked from one end of the alley to the other. A trampled mash of vegetation that had once been merrily blooming begonias slicked the black tar. A flush swept across my cheeks, raising a clammy perspiration in its wake.

"Son of a *whore!*" I shouted at the mess, scattering the cats in every direction, horizontal and vertical. A shudder ran the curve of my back, pausing for a ping between the shoulder blades. Swinging around to search for spying eyes, I heard the whoomp-whoomp-whoomp of pigeons' wings beating for the fire escapes, and the metallic clang of the door closing behind me. There was no sign of neighbors peering from the windows stacked piggyback on the back-facing alley. Still, I could not shake the conviction that there was someone lurking, maliciously appreciating my unease. It was some moments before the muscles in my legs obeyed the command from my brain.

I wandered, stupefied, through my devastated retreat. I knew it was not enthusiastic kitty sex that had toppled twenty yards of double-width brickwork, nor was it flak from the broken kitchen cabinets shattered over the asphalt. It required the purposeful strength of a man. A man with a mission. *The* man.

I strode back to the door, running a fine litany of verbal abuse through my mind—and stealing embarrassed glances over my shoulder.

Fixing the key in the lock I finally saw the note. It was stuck by gaffing tape just over the grimy lock.

NOTICE!
This area is private.
Unauthorized persons will be
prosecuted for trespassing.
EFFECTIVE IMMEDIATELY

The note was dated that day, and signed by "Classy Realty Management." A company with a mission. One owned in its entirety by Harvey Wood, landlord to the misbegotten. Well, I'd show him. I'd do what I had to do. I wasn't just some uneducated *schlub*. I knew my rights and I exercised them.

I gathered my things and cried all the way upstairs into my apartment.

Slasher had become so accustomed to my crying jags, he ignored me totally until I'd finished my symphony of oh-so-attractive hiccuping and nose blowing. He threw himself against my thigh and dozed off for the more lengthy talking-to-myself phase.

No doubt about it, Wood had every right to banish me from the back alley. I've voted Republican in my time. It was unequivocally *his* property to do with as he wishes.

But he never uses it for anything, my pathetic interior voice whined. Several times, I believe.

It was a wonder that I'd managed to hold on to access for as long as I did. At least he gave me warning.

Well, if Wood weren't such a cheap S.O.B., he would have changed the locks.

He shouldn't have to.

Yeah, well, he did it on purpose and I hate him.

So much for a mature attitude, Bowering.

Crying always makes me hungry, so I decided to grab something out of the refrigerator before plotting a just and hideous revenge. The light on my answering machine was blipping at me when I walked into the kitchen.

Yeah, yeah. Food first. People making me feel guilty and despicable, second. I opened the refrigerator door. The white interior was blinding. I suppose I'd been too depressed to go shopping. I plunked myself down on the floor, holding the door open with my foot, and stared at the hollow guts. There *was* an egg and some soy sauce. A new crack in the plaster crawled down my kitchen wall as I watched. Julio must have been doing floor tile. Feeling utterly bereft, I reached behind me and hit the Play button on my answering machine. What the hell. Might as well find out who else wanted to rip my face off.

Beep number one was from Barry, asking if I was feeling better.

I was not.

Beep number two was from the good sergeant Dan, asking if nine o'clock was too late to have dinner.

Not if I weren't hungry *now*. Not if he didn't mind having a date with a desiccated malnourishment case.

I let the refrigerator door close of its own volition and wandered to the bathroom to wash my face.

Beep number three was from Fran, bitching further about not getting Mr. Hillerman's apartment and wondering if I'd heard anything from the callback.

I had *not,* quelle surprise.

Number four was a hang up.

I sloshed cold (how novel) water on my face. Why does everyone wait for me to walk out of the apartment before phoning? Is it done on *purpose?* Am I that pathetic and depressing that people *arrange* to talk to my machine instead of me in person?

I blew my nose again during the beginning of number five.

"...contracts, if that's okay. Looking forward to it." Since I didn't take time to towel off, I dripped cold water back into the kitchen and the dreaded answering machine. The moment I hit the button to replay the messages, my frog phone gurgled.

"What?" I snapped into the frog belly cum mouthpiece.

"Congratulate me, Vic!" Fran ordered. Barry's voice played on tape from behind me.

"Congratulations, Fran. For what?" I could hear the second bleep and Dan's dulcet prerecorded tones.

"I *got* it!"

"Is it penicillin-resistant?" I could not resist. BEEP. Stereo. I had Fran to my ear, and Fran's voice from the beep monster. Very disorienting for a person in my nervous-collapse condition. I didn't ask her what "it" was, because if I heard it was Mame, I was reasonably frightened that I would start screaming and never be able to stop.

"No, Vic. I GOT THE MAME TOUR!"

Why are actors so loud?

Fran reiterated, just in case I'd gone deaf or something. "I got THE MAME TOUR!"

And so damned redundant? I heard the answering machine hang up on me for the second time. "Shush," I said, and then feeling guilty for not being a good sport, added, "Congratulations, that's wonderful, now hold on a sec." BEEP.

The machine babbled. "Victoria Bowering, this is Mike, stage manager for *Auntie Mame* and we'd like to..."

"So they offered me VERA. Is that GREAT?" Fran annoyed me further.

"GREAT goddammit!" I hissed, putting my ear directly to the machine.

"...offer you the role of Mame. We'll messenger the contracts over tomorrow morning. We need them signed and back to us by October thirtieth, at the latest. We discussed the money, so just get us the contracts, okay? Looking forward to it."

I sat. On Slasher as luck would have it, but he was agile and escaped with his life.

"And, of course, I'll be understudying Mame. Vic? Vic? Vic, are you still there?" Fran inquired over the phone.

"What?"

"Vic, are you all right?"

"Oh, I'm fine. Just fine. I was just listening to my messages, that's all. I JUST GOT THE MAME TOUR, TOO. *THAT'S ALL!*" I was not loud, I was "projecting."

"What?" Fran asked.

"I'M AUNTIE MAME! I'M EMPLOYED! MY LIFE HAS BEEN SAVED!" I projected with enthusiasm. "THANK YOU, GOD, THANK YOU, THANK YOU!" Suddenly, everything seemed a good deal rosier. Call me shallow.

"*You* got Mame?" Fran out-shallowed me by miles.

"YES, YES, YES, YES, YES! I'm MAME! Sorry about the understudying. As you know, I NEVER miss a performance." A cheap shot, but I couldn't resist. "Gotta go, Fran, talk to you later. I have to call everyone in the world." I hung up, swung Slasher into my arms and waltzed him around the room. I must say, he took it well. Salsa music bellowed over power tools from the heavens.

I then called everyone in the world.

My world, being New York and all, was not home to receive any of my calls, so I left messages on every answering machine in the world.

New Yorkers love their answering machines because they circumvent the annoying business of having their fascinating monologues interrupted. So I gushed, enthused, and generally was obnoxious, unencumbered by having to be polite or pretend to be even the slightest bit interested in what the other person had to say: sort of a one-woman show. During a lull in my marathon dialing, my friend Susie somehow got through to me. Being a New Yorker herself, she was taken somewhat aback when I personally, and not my advanced technology, answered the phone.

It took only a second for Susie to adjust and plunge ahead, "Vic! That's wonderful about the tour, and guess *what?*"

Just what I was afraid of: having to share dialogue. "What?" I asked, having been—in my mother's words—"drug up properly."

"ME, TOO!" she shrieked. "I'm going, TOO!"

Why are dancers so loud?

"You're kidding," I responded. More enthusiastically, I added, "That's GREAT! What are you doing?" I actually meant to sound happy. Despite having a body that won't quit, causing me all kinds of debilitating self-comparisons, Susie could always make me laugh and would be a terrific 'scum buddy' over the upcoming year. We'd done *Best Little Whorehouse in Texas* together for several months two years before. Every time I found my tampon/ underwear drawer frozen into a solid block of ice, I knew Susie would be around the corner laughing her perfect buns off. Not that she's competitive, but she played my maid in the show.

"I'M VERA CHARLES'S UNDERSTUDY," she burbled. "I'm FEATURED! Is that GREAT?"

I was swept along in the tidal wave of effusiveness, utterly blown away by how completely my miserable life had turned around. Two of my best friends in the universe would be along while I got my shot at the big time. Everything was perfect, absolutely perfect. I was going to have FUN for a change. I was going to be employed: employed in a job where—at the end of each evening—hundreds of people would applaud my work, whether they wanted to or not!

Classic Susie shot into gear. She thought, and so did I, that this kind of professional upswing called for a celebration. She said she'd take care of everything. All I had to do was present myself at McAleer's that night at eight o'clock. Cool. I knew she'd invite all the right people. Since only about 2 percent of actors actually ever get cast in paying jobs, we all know each other.

All that remained was to share my good fortune with the woman who—if God had a sense of humor—should have been my mother. Jewel LaFleur. If ever there were a day to suck down a bottle of champagne, this was it. Besides, the only construction in her building was two floors away. I could give my ears a rest.

I grabbed my keys, and an extra pack of cigarettes, leaving all my ennui in the back alley with the pureed begonias.

I'm so cute when I'm naive.

Everyone says so.

FOUR

That Afternoon

I KNOCKED MY special assigned code—knock-knock, wait, knock-knock-knock—on Jewel's apartment door so she would know it was me and not some inept rapist jiggling a key in her lock. Since I'd picked up a bottle of Château de Someplace-perhaps-in-Europe champagne and then the six-inch stack of mail and catalogs from her mailbox before arriving on her threshold, I was having some dexterity difficulty juggling the various piles. I was about to surrender and drop my burdens when the door opened.

"Here, darling," the elderly gentleman offered, "let me help you with all that." Mr. Feldstein, my sainted previous landlord, whipped the mail from under my arm, plucked the pack of cigarettes from my mouth, and placed them all on the end table next to "my" chair. He was close to ninety but had less trouble than I with such profoundly complicated items as stacks of envelopes. "Sit down, sit down," he gestured to the seat.

Jewel LaFleur, wearing a notably violet silk caftan trimmed in marabou feathers, was ensconced in her spot on the sofa and bent intently over an antique marble chessboard. I did as commanded, quietly sitting and clutching the cold bottle to my chest. After several minutes, Jewel spoke.

"Check and mate, Ben." She looked up and added, "You now owe me two hundred thirteen thousand, four hundred and twenty-two dollars. And Vic, don't cuddle the wine, you'll just whip up the sediment."

I got up and went over to my dear friend and kissed her cheek. Jewel doesn't get up. No one expects her to. After twenty-some years as one of New York's greatest strippers, she figured she'd moved quite enough already. As one of the smartest women I've ever met, I figured she must know. At seventy-something and three hundred some-odd pounds, she'd been housebound for at least the ten years I'd known her and had a better social life than I did. Richard Simmons, take note.

"What have we here?" Jewel asked, inspecting the bottle I'd brought. "Oh! How sweet. What's the occasion?"

"I GOT THE JOB!"

"Which job, sweetheart? Every Tom, Dick, and Myron in the city has been calling you back lately." She turned the bottle around to dubiously read the back label.

"MAME! I got the Mame tour!"

Mr. Feldstein came up beside me and kissed me gently on the forehead, saying, "Darling, how wonderful for you. Isn't that wonderful, Jewel?"

"It certainly is," Jewel agreed, shifting her great weight and smiling brilliantly. "Maybe this will get her to stop moping over what's-his-name, the law-yer who couldn't even shell out alimony."

"I didn't ask for any," I defended Barry for the thousandth time. Jewel ignored it, like everything she's heard too often to believe.

"We should have some champagne to celebrate." I started to take the bottle from her hand to carry to the kitchen and open, but she held firm and patted my cheek with her free hand. "No, sweetheart, you keep this and...put it on a salad or something. Ben, would you be a dear and open one of the bottles of Veuve Clicquot from the fridge?"

"This is no good?" I asked.

"That, sweetie, is panther piss." Mr. Feldstein returned in a flash with three glasses and an opened bottle of not-panther-piss. We toasted me, which doesn't happen nearly as much as I'd like. "To our darling, talented, beautiful, Victoria."

Someday I'm going to have to introduce Jewel to my mother to get some blood-relative pointers on keeping me from getting a swelled head. Then again...

"How are you doing, Mr. Feldstein?" I asked before taking a second mouthful of wine.

"At chess, not so good. My health, well, I'm older than Methuselah; I wake up, I say 'thank God.' But to be in the company of two such beautiful women, ah! Maybe I'm dead and gone to heaven." He smiled contentedly. Looking at his loving countenance, it was easy to remember the days when things like tenants' associations had not been necessary—when I didn't know the meaning of an MCI: broken things simply got fixed; and Mr. Feldstein was the father-figure to the entire Upper West Side. He was even a witness at Barry's and my wedding. Maybe I hated Harvey Wood most for not being Mr. Feldstein. As though hearing my thought, the old face clouded over. "I was sorry to hear about Sam Hillerman. A good man. Never caused any trouble in the thirty years he rented from me."

"He was very old," the platitude—almost a self-defense—sprung from my mouth.

"Ten years younger than me. He just gave up. No one seriously believes you had anything to do with it."

"It was cardiac arrest, Mr. Feldstein. The paramedics said so. I was there." I could hear the guilt in my own voice. The shame I felt hit me out of nowhere.

"Of course it was. Too much *tsuris*. Sam had to give up his home aide. Couldn't afford her anymore. My fault."

"Oh, get over it, Ben," Jewel scolded from behind her glass. "You said it. You're a thousand years old, sick, and so befuddled you can't even beat my ass at chess anymore, let alone manage six old buildings. No one blames you for selling. How could you know what kind of shit Wood is?" Mr. Feldstein shook his head wearily. Jewel held out her glass, which he refilled promptly, and spoke to me. "Of course, that's not to say Ben could beat my ass in his prime. He was senile thirty years ago, just like I am now. In the old days, I must have had a hundred spare sets of keys lying around for him because he was always leaving them somewhere. I was thrilled to death when he sold to Wood. Like to drove me crazy."

Mr. Feldstein laughed. "I just wanted an excuse to ring your bell and see you, Jewel." He turned to me and asked casually, "Didn't I leave keys with you, too, darling?"

I know a loaded question when I hear one.

"Not a full set." Not Mr. Hillerman's, I silently answered the unspoken query. Ivan's implication was right. Word travels fast and innuendo sticks like Velcro in the small town that constitutes the Upper West Side community.

"Probably even forgot to get them back to turn over to Wood."

I couldn't bring myself to be angry with Mr. Feldstein. "You remembered. Except for the garden key."

He looked at me with relief. "I guess I don't always forget, then, huh? Maybe I'm not ready for the grave quite yet."

"Hardly," I absolved him for doubting me.

"Still," he said, "things are not the way they were. Look at the people that *schmuck* allows to live here.

That *meshuggeneh* upstairs, poisoning poor little animals. What is the world coming to when a person can't even walk his dog?''

"What?'' I asked. "Who's poisoning dogs?''

Slasher—though only deluded in the belief that he was a dog—would scarf down anything that looked even remotely as if it would pass through his digestive tract: dust balls, spiders, plastic bags, cold sesame noodles.

"Oh, Loony Lucy, one floor up. Crazy as a shithouse rat. Everyone knows it.'' Jewel poured herself a tad more champagne and topped off mine. When I looked appalled, she reassured me. "Only dogs so far, dear. Slasher's safe as long as Lucy remains a specialist. The ASPCA told me she leaves little puddles of poison in tuna water by the apartment doors. The dogs take a swipe at it on their way to go outside. A few trips by, and the puppies are history. So don't take your cat on any walks.

"Neighbors don't look out for each other anymore; so many new faces. Nasty, but this *is* New York.''

"Can't the police do anything?'' I asked, horrified.

Mr. Feldstein answered for Jewel, who was sipping appreciatively again. "The police can't keep up with human murders, darling. We can't expect them to spend their time on—''

"—fidocide,'' Jewel finished, dryly. "Let's think about happier things. What are you going to wear for opening night, Vic? I think the Imperial Topaz set again. You look so well in it." She started rifling through a pile of gems and jewelry spilling off the side of her telephone table. "Oh, where the hell are they? Vic, check that table over there. You might have to dig some."

I opened the top drawer of an Empire sideboard that served as all-purpose junk drawer. But among the disemboweled pens and broken bones of paper were several satin jewelry cases. I recognized the aquamarine embroidered bag, lifted it from the flotsam and jetsam, and handed it to her.

"Yes!" Jewel smiled triumphantly, pulling the necklace, bracelet, and great dangling earrings from the case and dropping them in the middle of the chessboard. She wasn't called Jewel for nothing. The cantaloupe-colored gems winked from where they lay, provocatively splayed across black and white and black and white. Forty carats total weight, unless I missed my guess, which I wouldn't dare do in front of the woman who prided herself on teaching me everything I knew about fripperies I couldn't afford and no one else cared to purchase for me.

I protested, "Jewel, I couldn't take those on the road. They wouldn't be safe, all that time. We don't even open until after Christmas in San Francisco."

"Perfect! The pukkabrush will be dazzled!" She thrust the ornaments back into the bag and threw it at me. "Enjoy, for Christ's sake. Life is short and they're insured." I repressed my tears of gratitude, but my nose started to run. Someday I must figure out a way to express emotion without sniveling. "Now, you stop it, Vic, or I'll make you take the green tourmaline."

"Thanks, Jewel."

"Thank me by opening another bottle of champagne."

I did, but I just set it down on the carpet in front of Jewel. I kissed her again and said, "I have to go. The guys are having a party tonight at McAleer's to celebrate. I have to de-frizz my hair so everyone will remember me as better looking than I am. I wish the two of you could come. I promise you, someone will get stinking and take off his or her clothes. Very entertaining since you just *know* it'll be a dancer."

No, I don't know why actors are always making dancer jokes, except we do, and directors, producers, writers, choreographers, musical directors, and stage crews always laugh their butts off. Example: Why are tenor jokes always so short? So dancers can remember them.

"Darling, you know I don't go out anymore," Jewel demurred. "Hasn't been a damned thing I haven't seen a thousand times before going on out there. I don't mind staying inside. But when the dancer gets naked, call me on the phone so I can listen—and remember the good old days." Mr. Feldstein laughed heartily, and nodded comfortably.

"Mr. Feldstein?" I cajoled.

"We'll see, sweetheart. But don't be surprised if *I'm* the one running around naked." He stuck out his chest mockingly.

"I'd be delighted," I teased back.

Jewel waved me off, "You run along, Victoria. I think you're going to have to wash your hair and start all over to get the kinks out."

"I love you!" I said, meaning it more than actors often do. But just before I closed the door behind me, I added, "I almost forgot! There's a tenants' meeting tomorrow night at McAleer's, too. Jewel, I know you can't, but Mr. Feldstein, could you come? I know it's not your business anymore, but we could use your help in confirming some structural things in the buildings. Wood's trying to tell us we need a new hot-water boiler, and I know you put one in fourteen months ago. It'll be harder for him to lie with you in the room."

"Yes, darling, I'll be there. My friends are always my business. Now GO!" He shooed me off, and I shooed as instructed.

I SANG "You Gotta Have a Gimmick"—accompanied by a slew of appropriate bumps and grinds—down Jewel's hall stairs, out the building door, along the sidewalk, and to my tenement. Carlotta was re-organizing garbage cans between buildings and showed no particular amazement when I gave her a big hug and launched back into my solo performance. I did, however, scare the bejesus out of a rottweiler relieving himself on the BMW parked in front of the building.

In the old days, actors were forever running around the Upper West Side singing to themselves, and no one paid them the slightest attention. Since the neighborhood had yuppified there was less vocalization going on. People who could afford to live in the area by then seemed to have less *joie de vivre*. Even their dogs looked glum.

Perhaps glum is a by-product of anxiety generated via staggeringly escalating rents.

I hid Jewel's jewelry behind my sofa—I was about due for my semiannual burglary—and took a long, leisurely cold bath, until the guys working upstairs shut off the water. You can understand I wanted to be at the top of my form, which was substantially higher than it had been that morning.

I lay down on my back for an hour, hoping the places on my face that were about to have a birthday would settle back to where they originally belonged. During the six o'clock news, I chose my favorite Betsey Johnson black velour spandex minidress to wear. My old newly married boyfriend, Brad Sinclair, was on camera reporting live from Howard Beach, something about Joey Butafuoco again, but I couldn't hear very well over the banging of radiator pipes, courtesy of Terminator Julio. I couldn't say that it depressed me to see my ex-lover again, but it *did* remind me that I'd previously decided (in the initial flush of second rejection) that I must be getting too old for Betsey Johnson spandex dresses.

I tried on the hot little designer number anyway, discovered no untoward thirty-nine-ish-year-old places showing, and reconsidered my decision to start dressing as though I were the mother of three. To hell with Brad Sinclair. Auntie Mame wouldn't give a rat's ass for Brad Sinclair and his new ''little woman.'' I changed back into a white silk kimono to put on my makeup. Slasher looked a little disappointed that he wouldn't get the opportunity to shower the outfit with his own personal mark of ownership—his prodigious shedding.

I shamelessly admit to myself how much I enjoy every moment I spend in mindless primping. Maybe it's just *my* idea of perfect contentment that every evening when I'm preparing for a theater performance, sitting in front of my lighted mirror and applying the layers of stage makeup, I always think: I'm getting PAID to do play-pretend. I am actually getting a paycheck to sit here and put on false eyelashes. Damn, but life is good.

Still, it wasn't all *that* good that night. First, I loathe salsa music, a style of which the hearing-impaired Julio was obviously extremely fond. Second, the lying on my back to let my face settle hadn't worked any cosmetic miracles, so I resorted to one of those terrific actors' secrets, and applied an oil slick of hemorrhoid cream to my face before putting on the base foundation.

Of course, amateurs SHOULD NOT TRY THIS AT HOME. If the over-the-counter stuff "helps shrink the swelling of hemorrhoidal tissue," just imagine what it could do to an unsuspecting eyeball.

Before I knew it, two hours had been frittered away and it was eight o'clock. SHOW TIME! I couldn't wait to see everyone. *Everyone*.

Oops.

Dan was supposed to be coming over at nine o'clock. In my irresponsible enthusiasm mode, I taped a note over my door buzzer on the way out:

DAN!
CELEBRATION PARTY—MCALEER'S
Be there or be square.
Love, Mame

Dan Duchinski might be a little stubborn in the ethics department, but I had never had to explain my immaturity to him. Cops and semiprofessional fortune-tellers have a lot in common that way.

I couldn't wait to have him sweep me up in his arms and congratulate me. Maybe the thought of losing me for a year would throw him so off balance that I could take advantage of him. Maybe I could get him a little drunk. Maybe I wouldn't *have* to. I was one optimistic chick.

Did I mention how cute everyone says I am when I'm being naive?

FIVE

Same Evening

WHEN IT COMES TO parties, unemployed actors do not adhere to the "fashionably late" school of civilized thought. McAleer's was already bopping with ebullient thespians by the time I arrived. My excellent spirits were further buoyed by the fact that there were some unknowns in evidence, proving that what Duchinski always said—that I was on a first-name basis with every dubious character on the Upper West Side—was untrue. Some of the unfamiliar may have been just regular evening customers, but when performers party, everyone's a soon-to-be-pal. Also, McAleer's jukebox was set at a lower decibel level than my apartment for a change. My eardrums uncrimped.

Susie had positioned herself by the entrance. She was wearing a Betsey Johnson spandex dress, too. Smaller, of course. Shorter, naturally. More vibrant, as would be expected. I forgave her. She was my *understudy*. We did the requisite hugging and kissing, as well as some sedate jumping up and down and complimenting one another. All according to the book. It was like an upbeat episode of Oprah Winfrey. I felt back on the road toward mental health.

A blond guy was standing at the bar making balloon animals. He was kind of cute, and I was in the mood for a diva present (that's any gift that costs less than a dollar), no matter how insipid, so I sidled up next to him to order my Rolling Rock. Never mind, I caught myself, my Genesee.

I was too old for blondie by ten years, but the light was bad, so I dared to venture my "Golly, you don't look that old," and moderately interested look at his skillful manipulation of latex. Fran's face poked from behind the tallish, thinnish man with the receding hairline to my right. She shouted my name and rushed over. We performed the same talk-show ritual Susie and I had accomplished at the door: huggy-kissy, "you look great!"

Ivan, the bartender, was still on duty, and busy. On one of his sweeps past, he leaned in between the blond and the balding and asked, "Usual, Vic?" I nodded, not quite knowing what the usual was, since McAleer's no longer carried my old usual, but Ivan didn't pause to notice. I threw three singles down on the bar, hoping that would cover whatever it was that I was served. McAleer's had become a theater hangout in the days of brewskis-for-a-quarter, but those days were as dead as Laurence Olivier. A beer of some sort appeared before me.

"Vic," Fran interrupted my trot down Memory Lane, "this is Pat Arnold." She nudged the young blond man. "He's a juggler. And this," she put her hand on the other unfamiliar man's shoulder so that

I would absolutely understand the territorial parameters, "is D. L. Blacker. D.L.'s a lawyer." Fran intoned the "L" word as though she were saying the rosary. Not that Fran and I are competitive, you understand.

Since I had already been married to an attorney and was never a fan of either mimes or circus performers, the bloom was off *that* rose, and most definitely took Blacker and Arnold out of the flirtation running for me. I'm a slow healer, I guess. Nonetheless, we shook hands all around, and Pat offered to make me a balloon doggie. I wanted a giraffe with an apple stuck in its throat, but graciously accepted the stupid pink poodle. A familiar voice interrupted the fatuous compliments I was about to make over the miraculously appearing bulb at the end of the balloon tail.

"I never knew pink was your color, Vic," Brad Sinclair, the newlywed newsman, crooned from behind me. To hear such a comment from a man who'd taken me to dinner one night and was honeymooning the next in Puerto Vallarta with someone else might have offended my dignity, but as an actor, I was truly blessed not to have had any in the first place. Still, I was ready to inflict serious bodily injury on whichever *dancer* had invited Brad.

That would have been Susie, of course.

I reminded myself that I had recently become a star, and that such violent behavior would be perceived as beneath me. Fortunately, as an actor, just about nothing is in fact, technically, beneath me.

I magnanimously forgave her lapse, but Susie's tampon and underwear drawer had, from that moment on, my name and Frigidaire's written all over it.

"Brad!" I enthused, trying to spot his new wife without appearing to—which we all know is impossible. "I thought you were working tonight."

"Glad to hear you're still tuned in to Big Apple News." He cleared his well-known throat. "I've been meaning to call."

Really? I didn't say. After only two MONTHS, you would do *that* for *me?* Just because I innocently turned on the tube one night to check the weather, and instead heard your WEDDING announcement. From Geraldo Rivera, for Christ's sake. I also did not add, why ever would you feel you should CALL? Would a woman in my tragically low-self-esteem bracket need REASSURANCE of her desirability under those circumstances?

I smiled benignly, patiently, appearing only mildly interested, rather like Deborah Kerr as a nun in *Heaven Knows, Mr. Allison.*

Susie was most emphatically going to be paying for this one. Vaseline in her Nexus hair-care products, perhaps. I would have come up with something more heinous, but Barry arrived—looking so damned adorable I wanted to smack him—and elbowed his way to my side.

My personal thinning lawyer nodded at Fran's thinning lawyer on my right and tersely said, "Blacker."

Very *L.A. Law*.

Blacker nodded back and said, "Laskin."

Very *Law and Order*.

Oh, joy. A personality conflict already. I sucked down half of my Genny, or whatever it was. Brad and Barry shook hands like friends, though all they had in common was the fact that they were the only two men in the room who knew for an absolute fact that I'm a real redhead, even naked. Ivan set a Guinness in front of Barry without being asked, and Brad ordered a martini.

I'd always suspected that Susie had my address book Xeroxed when my back was turned.

McAleer's was rapidly filling up to the dart board with my lurid past. The atmosphere was deteriorating, from a going-away party straight into "get-out-of-town." I made up my mind.

Visine in Susie's tofu one half hour before show time.

"Excuse me," I apologized to the men, moving away from the bar, "it's getting a little close for comfort here."

Fran's hand shot up from behind Blacker and eagerly tata'ed me off. I'd forgotten she was there. I bumped and sidled my way through the mass of people until I located a marginal oxygen supply. Brad and Barry followed with their drinks, just as though either one of them deserved to breathe. Yes, I was slipping: taking things personally again.

Barry shouted to me over the blare of the jukebox. "I got a fax of your contract from the producers, Vic. I thought you said the money was good. Anyway," he didn't wait for a defense from me, "you'll be okay as long as you can get a long-term sublet."

Shit. I hadn't even thought about that.

I asked if he was sure. Of course he was, he's the man who does my taxes and used to pay my MasterCard bill.

I asked if he would take Slasher in case I couldn't line anyone up before I had to leave town. He certainly couldn't; he had a "friend" with allergies. I should have known there would be trouble in River City. The two people I counted on to Slasher-sit—Fran or Susie—were going on the road with me. Damn.

"I'll find someone," I brazened it out. Damn!

Ivan was circulating, picking up beer pitchers and glasses. "No doubt in my mind," he said, dumping the ashtray Brad held in his left hand into a plate of chicken wing bones. Ivan looked Barry and Brad slowly over and smirked. Testosterone gas billowed from all three men. I was getting claustrophobic again.

"Vic needs someone to sublet, Igor," Barry said, handing Ivan his empty glass dismissively.

"Perfect. How much and how long?" Ivan asked.

"Five hundred a month, I bite the utilities, you pick up the cat food," I leaped. "One year minimum."

"Done," Ivan said smoothly, shaking on it with me. "Another round?" he inquired of Barry, and then Brad. "My treat. I'll send the waitress by."

When Ivan became lost in the mob, Barry glared at me. "How *could* you do that? You don't even know him."

Brad concurred, "He could be anybody. I cover stories like this all the time. He could be some kind of mass murderer. What about Slasher's safety?"

"You always hated Slasher," I countered evenly. "Besides, I have feelings about these things. I happen to be a very good judge of character."

Cool, huh? This spoken from a woman standing between two men who had run off with other, shorter, women. The truth is, when it comes to anything but my love life, I have excellent instincts. It's one of the talents that have made me the high-priced bar mitzvah fortune-teller I have been forced to be upon occasion. But as insurance, I made myself swear to ask Timmy the bartender about his co-worker later.

Nonetheless, I felt stupid as a bucket of hair. Before it could show too much on my face, my personal space got even smaller.

Susie appeared with two men in tow. One was a medium-sized swarthy gentleman in a staggeringly pricey suit; the other was Dan Duchinski, who was either glowering, or tired. I couldn't tell. A heavyset law-enforcement type raised a glass to him as he passed.

"Sergeant Duchinski," he toasted.

"Lieutenant Longreen," Dan scowled and joined me. I didn't even ask what *that* soap opera was about.

The dark mustached fellow turned out to be a Lebanese real estate developer, I couldn't hear a word he said, and I made a mental note to ask Barry if I could sue Wood for a violation of some environmental factor that caused me irreparable hearing impairment.

Mercifully, before I could respond in a totally inappropriate way to a conversation I couldn't hear, I was dragged over to the piano to sing my "signature" song, "Peel Me a Grape." It's everything you might suspect it to be. Susie sang her specialty, "The Masochism Tango," which is probably *more* than you suspect it to be, and the rest of the evening passed in a blur of camaraderie and excitement. Sort of what had been intended in the first place. Ivan kept my glass filled, so I ended up a bit sloshed, which was *not* intended.

At two o'clock in the morning, Dan took my arm and led me out of the bar.

The air outside was crisp as an apple, blowing gently off the Hudson river and carrying a pleasant saltiness. I hadn't worn a coat, since my apartment was so near McAleer's, but it was cool enough that I

shivered in the breeze. Dan wrapped a large, warm
arm around me. I put my hand around his waist and
pressed my body against his side—and the gun that
was strapped to it. There is no more soothing way to
walk the streets of New York at two in the morning
than in the company of a really big man packing a
legal sidearm. I assured myself I didn't need any old
attorney husband. Not then.

The significance of my life change had settled in at
last. No more cloying money trouble, Slasher cared
for, a chance to advance myself professionally and
get away from all the demoralizing things that simply weren't working out: Barry, Brad, the tenants'
association. There is a calm that descends over a
performer who is leaving town for a job. It's a total
and perfect giving over of responsibility. The lines
are broad, clear, and restrictive. Relief. Work. It was
more than time for me to rely on myself. Mr. Hillerman's windows were dark at last. Peace reigned in
Gotham.

In the apartment, I asked Dan if he wanted a de-
caf. Habitual wife-behavior is hard to break. I took
his grunt to mean "yes" and went to the kitchen to
make the coffee. I could hear him shrug off his jacket
and heave Slasher onto his big chest.

"Is that a good boy?" Dan asked the cat. "*What*
a good boy." I peeked around the door to see Slasher
gently bite Dan's nose. Duchinski allowed the cat to
crawl up under his sweater and nod off to a snoring
sleep, cradled on a cop arm. Lucky feline.

I put the mugs of coffee onto the cocktail table and tucked myself under Dan's free arm. Slasher was purring so intensely, I could feel the reverberations up the downy contour of Dan's skin. It was an appropriate time for quiet sweet-talking, but I didn't seem to have the inclination.

More's the pity; Dan did. He stroked Slasher through the cop's sweater as I drowsed.

"It's not flying, Vic." My heart bolted; I did not move. I lectured myself not to project the scenario, but the party fortune-teller in me couldn't help it. Dan's deep voice cut through my ever-eager internal schizophrenia. "One of the first things I learned when I became a cop was that I can't change the world. I hated it, Vic, but it was the most important lesson a cop learns. Later—after getting slammed a couple of times—I understood that I would never have the power to change an individual human being, either. Much later I figured out that there's a lot about *me* that makes me try—no matter how futile—to make everything 'all right.' I'm just a plain cop, Vic."

I knew that. I liked that. Why did I smell a "but"? Why did I have to hear one, tonight of all nights?

"You, baby, somehow—damned if I know when—started to make me forget that," Dan droned mechanically. I shifted position, but he held me close so I couldn't look into his face. Dan adjusted Slasher paternally beneath his clothing. "I'm crazy about you and the boy here, too." Somehow I knew better than to speak. Dan continued, "The operative word in that sentence being 'crazy.' I don't *think* when I'm around you, Vic. My brain doesn't work. I put up with the men all over the place, the nutzoid actors, the traveling and the temperament. My brain is gone. Ordering in Chinese food for a cat?" Dan cradled Slasher closer and took a noisy breath. "I can't make you do what I want anymore than I could train The Slash to be Rin Tin Tin. I thought I knew better than that. I've got reality shoved down my throat every day of my life. I *believed* I had the concept nailed, Vic." He expelled air. "But I just *don't*. Big, old, tough Dan Duchinski could not make you divorced. Okay. But"—there was the *but*—"I can't deal with you being married, either. And here's the funny part—I finally wake up and figure out that I can't wait anymore, like a good cop. Not *for* you or to *have* you."

"Dan..."

"No, Vic, I can't do it anymore. I'm all about being the big guy, and wanting what I can't have makes me puny. I see you with Barry and I want to grind him into compost." He would not let me move, and I so very much wanted to see his FACE. "And, oh God," he laughed, "you don't think I didn't know about Brad Sinclair, do you? I actually ran him through the—" I could physically feel Dan's bitter humiliation as he struggled to finish. "That's it." Dan stood. Slasher dropped indignantly out of the bottom of the warm sweater to the floor. "You can't do what you can't do. Okay. It's really okay. But neither can I.''

As he grabbed his jacket from the Lincoln rocker, I fumbled over Slasher to my feet. I still had not seen Dan's face. He had the door open before I could reach his arm. He shook me off so violently, I stumbled backward. Not until then did he look at me. Though the sockets were rimmed with crimson, his eyes were absolutely dry in their self-disgust.

My self-disgust doesn't work that way, dammit. He swept a tear from my cheek with his meaty hand and examined it, as though he could discover what chemical poison had reduced him to such a pathetic level.

''I...'' the words caught in his throat. ''Let's be grown-ups here.'' He leaned over, hand on the doorknob, and kissed me so gently I might have mistaken the caress for the flutter of a small sparrow past my lips. ''If there're anymore problems with the Hillerman business, maybe you should call Barry.''

The door shut behind him and I heard his final farewell, ''See you around, Slasher, old boy. Try to kick that sesame noodle monkey on your back.''

And there I was. Just like *that*. Balanced back on the slick rim of misery. Just when you think you've seen it all coming, well, you haven't.

Exhausted, I didn't bother to drag myself to the bed I'd never shared with Dan. Leaving town was going to be more than just my professional salvation.

When the world is collapsing around you, run for your life and figure it all out, later.

Thank you, Scarlett O'Hara.

SIX

THAT NEXT MORNING, I stood in the back alley, wearing the clothes I'd slept in, staring emptily at my shattered garden, and pondering the unflagging consistency of shitty karma.

To be less florid, I was feeling very sorry for myself, indeed.

I ran every positive visualization I could conjure up through my mind to remind myself that—except for my absolute inability to transfix any one male of the species for longer than fifty-seven seconds—my, pardon my use of the word, "life" was in better shape than it had been in years.

On the downside, the misery I was feeling could not be bemoaned to any of my actor friends, who would be thunderstruck that any minor personal devastation would distract me in the slightest from professional success. The alley cats wove, not trusting but hopeful, in and around my meandering, dodging the trajectile moldings and flooring that sailed from poor, dead Mr. Hillerman's back window.

In unison, my and forty feline necks stretched suddenly skyward. Forty-one pairs of ears strained for a phantom noise down the alley that never came. If my gut feelings were not so reliable—and the cats didn't confirm them at that moment—I would have cheerfully taken that moment to book my reservation at Château Weird. The cats slowly regained mobility. I waited in morbid certainty.

The garden door opened languidly, spilling even more darkness into the channel between brick monoliths. I set my jaw and rooted, heart brazenly thundering.

A left hand crept deliberately around the edge of the exterior molding.

Mr. Feldstein joined me, saying, not chastising, "You left the outside door unlocked, darling." He looked at me, forehead wrinkling. "Oh, my poor sweetheart, what *happened?*"

Now, if there's one thing I can't deal with during an emotional collapse, it's empathy. I blew out the breath I'd been holding, and crumbled like a good pie crust.

Though shorter than me and frail as a spray of baby's breath, Mr. Feldstein put his arms around my back, pulled my head to his shoulder, and whispered rhythmically—over and over, "Shush, shush, shush. Everything's going to be all right. Shush, shush, shush. Nothing's worth these tears." We sat on twin outcroppings of brick rubble out of Julio's pitching range, Mr. Feldstein holding my hand. "What else? What is it, darling? What could be so bad?"

I stopped sniveling long enough to say, "I'm just being a baby."

"So go ahead. Get it all out, and then you can go back to being the czarina of all the Russias."

I'll admit it; I smiled, tears running all over my face. Mr. Feldstein handed me a linen handkerchief. I wiped. I blew. I felt better. I got angry.

"Oh, Mr. Feldstein, I have a million things to do. I have to figure out what clothes to take with me for a year on the road. I don't know what I'm going to want to wear next August. I have to clean out at least half of my drawers and closet space for my sublettor—who may be a psychotic ax-murderer. It's too much; I'm too old for this anymore. I highlighted my lines in the script and I have so many monologues it looks like a dog pissed on the pages. Mr. Feldstein, I haven't had a legit theater job in so long, I'm not sure I can *learn* all those words anymore." I blew my nose again, for emphasis. "And I'm leaving in the middle of a mess with Wood over phoney MCIs and Jewel's fighting eviction. She has *always* been there for me, and now I'm just going to *leave* her. Who's going to help Jewel?"

"I will, darling." I must have looked doubtful because he continued, "If worse comes to worse—and it won't—I still own a little building on the East Side with room for Jewel. Now, that's our secret, just in case. Promise?"

"I promise."

"But darling, I used to be the landlord, and I know it is virtually impossible to evict anyone—even psychotic ax-murderers—in so little time as a year. You'll be back in plenty of time to protect your friend. But, between you and me, our Jewel needs no protection. You should play chess with her sometime. She's a *killer*."

That made me feel a bit better, but a sigh escaped my lips anyway. "I missed poor Mr. Hillerman's funeral this morning. Someone from the old days should have been there."

"I was there, darling, and Jewel sent flowers."

One of the construction crew dumped an ashtray outside into the breeze. For a moment, it looked as though the sky were giving up acid snow. A crushed butt rolled in our direction and the alley cats dashed forward to see if it was edible. I sighed.

"He ruined my garden. Wood did. It was so pretty." I kicked the orphaned cigarette butt away. "I shouldn't be here." I pointed to the sign on the door. "He's posted the area."

"And so what else?"

"And I have a birthday coming up on Halloween."

"And?"

Might as well.

"Dan walked out on me."

"Ah."

I stood and walked to the cinder-block wall that separated my back alley from the landscaped garden of the bankrupted co-op building that loomed behind, and smashed my hand, flatfisted, onto the gritty cement. I slapped it repeatedly. Gravel embedded in the wall scraped furrows on my palms and knuckles. Pigeons flew, and cats scurried. Only Mr. Feldstein remained calm. He took my arm and led me out of the backyard, up through the basement, making sure the exterior door was secured, and up the stoop stairs to my apartment.

He patted my by-then bleeding hand and advised, "Put some antiseptic on those cuts. Then you take a long, hot bath, then a nap. Don't worry about the meeting tonight. I'll be there. All your friends will be there."

"Almost. Not one of them."

"Then what a lucky girl you are to have enough that one can be missing and still leave a crowd."

Kissing his cheek with gratitude, I went inside and did as instructed. Except it was like trying to sleep through the clamor of the Tet Offensive. And that "hot" part of the bath thing. I figured I could use some cooling down, anyway.

BLAHHHHHHHHHHHHHHHHHHHHHHHHHT,   The screeching of the intercom buzzer startled me so completely that I threw the towel I was drying myself with into the now-listing ceiling fan. At least it wasn't turned on, a pleasant coincidence for a change.

BLAHHHHHT. BLAHHHHHHHHHT. I threw on a silk
robe and dashed to the door before BLAHHHHHHH-
HHHHHHHHHHHHT I had to hear that sound again. The
only thing I can compare the noise to is the feeling
you get when you bend a fingernail back to the
knuckle. I opened my peephole to try and peer
through the BLAHHHHHHT darkness of the hall to see
who was ringing BLAHHHHHHT me from the
BLAHHHHHHT vestibule. I BLAHHHHHHHHHHH-
HHHHHT couldn't, and hit the door release button
before my head exploded, still squinting through the
little security window. The outline shadow of a man
opened the Folsom Prison door and entered, his
head turning to check the apartment numbers on the
doors along the hallway. Ultimately, he found
apartment E—me. Even with his nose directly at the
peephole, the darkness was so absolute that I
couldn't recognize him. I belted my robe.

"Who is it?" I shouted through the metal door.

"Omar."

"Who?" Actors adore playing these little decep-
tions. I, personally, have called friends and identi-
fied myself as Elizabeth Tudor. But in this instance I
didn't recognize the voice and wasn't in the mood to
play peekaboo with some chorus boy out of my
checkered past.

"Omar Salim." Still no bells of recognition ringing in the clock tower of my brain. "I believe we have
a lunch scheduled for today, do we not?"

Oh, shit. It was the Lebanese chap Susie had introduced me to the night before at McAleer's. A real estate something-or-other. Damn. Aside from Julio and the boys being on lunch break, I was on a true bad-karma roll. And, of course, probably everyone from Ninety-sixth Street to Times Square knew about the date except me.

One last inspection to be sure nothing untoward was poking out of the kimono, and I sheepishly opened the door.

"Please come in, Mr. Salim," I stepped back to allow him past, all the while wondering what the punishment was for being seen wearing my present attire in a Muslim country. Not that Salim was necessarily Muslim. Or Orthodox. Or, oh shit. "Please excuse my appearance, I'm afraid I don't, well, it's been a, well, I may have forgotten," I finally admitted.

Very smooth, huh?

"You look delightful," Omar insisted, and held out an impressive bouquet of eighteen stems of Casablanca lilies secured with a length of pale pink satin ribbon. I don't know how I could have missed it when he walked in. The arrangement was a full foot and a half in diameter and as fragrant as a toppled bottle of good perfume. "If I am early, I would be happy to come back at a more convenient time."

"No, no," I protested the way I do when trying to convince some idiot who has called me at three-thirty in the morning that I am not, in fact, asleep. It's that old New England training, I guess. "Let me put these in water. Please, have a seat." I dashed off to the kitchen to try to find a suitable vase, knowing that never in my wildest imaginings would I ever own a container that would qualify as suitable. "May I offer you something?" I quickly surveyed my assortment of orphan liquor bottles and the echoing interior of the refrigerator. "I can offer you, uh, peach schnapps, bourbon, or soy sauce."

Don't you just *hate* it when you know you're out of your league?

"If it's not too much trouble," Salim said from the doorway, where he was watching me with some amusement, "I would very much like a cup of tea." He was really quite handsome, I noticed. Not terribly tall—who is?—but about five-foot ten, lovely symmetrical features, intelligent brown eyes, and a perfectly manicured full mustache. In my opinion, all men should wear facial hair. If God had wanted men to be clean-shaven, he wouldn't have given them a secondary sexual characteristic. He was a spiffy dresser, too: Harris Tweed and gray flannel. Cashmere turtleneck, white.

The only obvious flaw that occurred to me was his English: a slight Gallic accent, but otherwise an annoyingly more extensive vocabulary than mine.

"No trouble at all." While I fussed awkwardly, Slasher jumped to the top of the refrigerator near the kitchen doorway and stuck his face directly into Omar's. Slasher's tongue swiped exploratorily over the man's nose, but no love bite. Both Slasher and I were trying to behave properly for a change, I guess. Of course, at least Slasher was dressed, unlike me.

"What a lovely animal," Salim commented, lifting the cat into his arms and stroking him. "What breed is he?"

I set the water to boil, and leveled, "Felinus Domesticus Vulgaris." Salim laughed full out, behavior that I generally like in response to a witticism, though I do not, under any circumstances, expect it. "If you'll excuse me, I'll let you and Slasher get acquainted while I . . .

BLAHHHHHHHHHHHHHHHHHHHHHHHHHHHHHHHH-HHHHHHHHHHHT.

". . . get the door."

"Of course."

Salim stepped aside, examining the decor—or whatever it is that I have—and patting the cat. I had just made it into the living room when the door opened, spewing Harvey Wood like a wad of spit into my previously tidy space.

"Pardon me?" I sputtered, ever the product of my upbringing.

"You and me should have a talk." Wood took off his jacket and slung it onto the sofa. His curious stare violated the corners of the room. "Did a nice job with the place, Bowering. Victorian, right? Like your name? Nice."

"Thanks," I recovered. I picked up Wood's jacket and handed it to him. "We can talk tonight at the tenants' meeting."

"Not the way we can talk here," Wood answered. "I think you are ignoring how easy I can make your life in this apartment." I'll admit it, I was too shocked even to lift the amazing levitating Bowering eyebrow. "There's been some talk about Sam Hillerman's untimely demise. Got a call. Told the fuzz you took care of the old fart out of the goodness of your heart. Naturally, NYPD doesn't hold much with that kind of sentiment."

"You're kidding."

"Don't have time; won't even pretend. It's time we made nice, Victoria. Since you're so civic-minded, my good nature might even slop over onto your neighbors." He reached for the belt of my robe. "Ya never know."

I stepped back, too outraged to yell, which is what happens with us New Hampshire girls. We generally have to plan in advance for spontaneous reactions that might be construed as in some way rude.

I said, all the while planning, "I think not." There was that Deborah Kerr thing again. It's a reflex. "Why don't you just get out of my face?" That's better: Bette Midler. "I leave in a week, *Mr.* Wood, and I'll be out of your scalp for a year. Consider it a sabbatical. You can leave your future innuendos with Ivan, the six-foot, five-inch guy who's subletting."

"Oh? Have I approved your sublet, Missy? As president of the tenants' association, I'm sure you're aware that you can't sublet *my* apartment without my *written* permission."

"Which cannot be unreasonably withheld," I retaliated swiftly, beginning to regain my stride.

"What a shame that Housing Court is so backed up. *Eventually* I'm sure everything will be decided according to the rules and guidelines of the New York City Housing Commission. And how inconvenient that your unwanted upstairs neighbor croaked in an apartment that your best friend was pissing herself to get ahold of." He crossed his arms. "I got the time, I got the lawyers."

More spontaneous than the whole body, my hand flew up from my side, trying to decide whether to be a claw or a fist. Wood caught it easily, and applied enough pressure to my wrist to turn coal to diamonds. Smiling, he threw down my arm and advised, "Think about it, Bowering. I have you by the short hairs, and don't you *ever* forget it."

Omar and Slasher entered quietly from the rear of the apartment. Slasher said nothing. Salim coolly reiterated my deflected message to Wood.

"I believe the lady would prefer that you leave now, Sir."

Wood might be pond scum, but not a dummy. He was not about to tangle with a man armed with a sleeping cat. The landlord's eyes did a once-over of

Salim, and then a longer one of my bare feet and bathrobe.

"Sorry, Bowering," Wood thrust at the door, opening it, "didn't mean to interrupt you while you're 'working.' I'll catch you tonight when you're off duty. Gotta return a call to a homicide detective, anyway."

I don't know how the lead crystal candy dish and cover got into my hand. I do know how it shattered against the metal door frame, spitting M&M's and Hershey's Kisses (with almonds) all over the living room. Just call me deadeye.

"That SON OF A BITCH!" I railed in frustrated fury, along with an extended string of other colorful colloquialisms I sincerely hope were never taught wherever Omar learned his English.

Omar waited for the verbal storm to pass and the impotent crying to commence before asking, "Excuse me, but where do you keep your vacuum cleaner?" I pointed to the hall closet. He got out the small canister and plugged it into the wall socket. Slasher danced around the Arab's feet as he sucked candy and glass shards into the machine. Omar would run the vacuum over an area, move Slasher out of the way, vacuum, move Slasher. I watched, mute, unashamed that a man I didn't even really know was cleaning up my tantrum. When the floor was safe, he inquired, "How ever did you make the cat unafraid of the noise of the machine?"

"I don't know" was my incisive reply. I took the hose from Omar's hand, turned the canister back on, and ran the upholstery attachment over Slasher's belly. "He likes being vacuumed. I got him out of the alley when he was about two. Who knows what kind of warped kittenhood he survived."

Finally embarrassed by the accidental recurrence of my not-a-nervous-collapse, I put the vacuum cleaner away and microwaved water to replace that which had boiled away, unattended on the stove, for tea. I served in my good English bone-china service, which I hope redeemed me, somewhat.

It was lucky that we both drink our tea black. Soy sauce is innovative, but not much of a thrill in Earl Grey.

After my profuse apologies to Salim, we decided to put off lunch for another day. It was beginning to look as if I were going to be trapped in the neighborhood for some time—and very much in need of a free lunch. I believe I did an admirable job of being a good hostess, considering I was livid with rage and hysterical at my entrapment at the hands of Harvey Wood.

"If you don't mind my mentioning it," Omar mentioned it, "I cannot help but notice how...agitated you have become. If it is not presumptuous of me, would it be possible for me to attend this meeting you are having this evening? I have some experience in legal residential matters and would be most happy to assist, if at all possible."

"That's very kind of you," Deborah Kerr answered. She also told him the location and the time, and walked him to the door, just like a woman not having a nervous breakdown.

Then she took a Valium and a nap.

And dreamed of no one. Only of being alone.

SEVEN

That Evening, October 24

THERE WAS AN orange-and-white EMS van blocking the sidewalk when I left for the tenants' association meeting. Several extremely good-looking firemen reassured me that there was no gas leak that was going to level the area, nor an insidious slow-burning fire expected to reduce my home to ashes during my absence.

I wanted to ask them why firemen as a group are so much better looking than all other municipal employees, but I was running late, and New York's Bravest were already watching me as though my elevator didn't run all the way to the penthouse.

Kerry McAleer, scion to the fabulous McAleer fortune, had set up chairs behind the crimson velvet restraining rope he'd been forced to buy since the bar had become a pit stop of the Bridge-and-Tunnel weekend bacchanalia.

This—for those of you who live in America and not New York City—is a bizarre sociological ritual where hundreds of marginally legal out-of-town drinkers stand in line for hours waiting for admittance to a pub crammed like a Japanese subway full of other people just like them, whom they could have met at the mall if they'd only stayed in New Jersey.

Go figure the contemporary Pop Culture.

The three seats for the tenants' steering committee were set up facing the neat rows and the entrance to the bar. The dart board would be located directly above my curly head. If the concept hadn't been so ludicrously perfect, I would have asked someone to move it. Not as yet suicidal, I did have the dart cabinet locked tight, however. Call me craven.

Slightly more than a dozen tenants had already taken their seats. Mr. Feldstein was the only participant in the first row, though. By quarter past the scheduled starting time, the chairs were full. Omar arrived, made a pit stop for a snifter of brandy and a *tête-à-tête* with Ivan, who was manning the bar, and took a place next to Mr. Feldstein. I introduced the two men, who immediately started chatting like old drinking buddies. An Arab and a Jew. Maybe I should have looked into a career in the diplomatic service. Barry plunked himself down on the other side of Mr. Feldstein.

Cochairperson Fran took her seat to the left of the target, and my other friend and cotarget, Michelle, to the right. Righteously indignant once again, I took the hot seat and called the meeting to order. Stragglers picked up drinks from the bar and stood behind the early birds. Ivan handed his bar rag to the genuine British barmaid and joined the cluster.

The only person not in evidence was Don Juan Wood. Even Loony Lucy had come, though no one carrying liquid refreshment dared to sit next to her. On the other hand, I couldn't help but notice a few askance glances in my direction, as well.

We discussed the trees it had taken me three years to finagle from the city that were planted in the sidewalk in front of the buildings. The tenants without exception hated the varietal I'd chosen and wondered why I didn't bother to take a few more seconds to have tree guards installed. I explained that we had precisely eleven dollars and twenty-seven cents in the association fund, which was not enough to buy a roll of chicken wire—let alone tree guards—and that those who wanted to invest another three years of *their* time could order up ginkgoes for all I cared.

The tenants then wanted to know if the eleven dollars and twenty-seven cents was being held in an escrow account for security reasons. Michelle explained that she kept it hidden in her junk-food drawer at her office.

Loony Lucy demanded an independent accounting and documentation of all communal moneys. It was her opinion that I had embezzled the funds in order to bankroll my extensive plastic surgery.

I opined—with admirable restraint, if you don't mind my saying so—that I wished I looked that rested.

Mr. Feldstein took the opportunity to go to the pay phone beside the double kitchen doors, punch in a

credit card number, dial a shorter sequence, and then
left the receiver to dangle in air before returning to
his seat.

"Didn't want Jewel to miss this," Mr. Feldstein
said, lowering himself slowly. The tenants applauded. Loony Lucy ranted for a while about un-
conscionably special treatment for people like
unrepentant strippers who don't deserve it when she
was being maliciously robbed of her right to move
into Mr. Hillerman's apartment. She wondered aloud
if I were using the space to store drugs, and then
swerved off into an abbreviated diatribe about
Communists putting fluoride in the drinking water.

In the middle of an especially vituperative pas-
sage, Brad Sinclair made his appearance and held the
door for the last latecomer, Harvey Wood. Brad
went for a martini, Wood went directly for my
throat.

The landlord ambled to face the tenants, standing
directly in front of me. Why, oh why, did I have them
lock the dart case?

"Just wanted to know who'd show up tonight,"
Wood examined each person. "Half, maybe." He
walked to the rear and took root next to Ivan, whose
amused smirk never wavered. I suppose Wood found
the agitated whispering gratifying. I lit a cigarette:
another reason to hold tenants' meetings in a bar.

Usually, the times one most needs a cigarette is
where it's strictly prohibited—hospitals, airplanes,
funerals, and medallion cabs. I was in that New

Hampshire place again where I couldn't get a word past my lips. I missed Dan.

I wanted his gun.

Mr. Feldstein stood shakily, leaning heavily on his cane, and faced the people who now lived in the buildings he once owned. His legs might have been weak, but his voice carried easily over the noise of the barroom.

"I am Ben Feldstein, and most of you know me from the old days. I have owned residential buildings here in the city for, well, I inherited them from my father, so it's been a long time. I believe there's a reference to the date somewhere in the Dead Sea Scrolls, but correct me if I'm wrong." The audience tittered. I wondered if Mr. Feldstein had ever been an actor. He went on, "I know a landlord's rights. I also know a landlord's obligations."

"RENT STRIKE!" Loony Lucy shouted. No one even turned to look at her—not that it would have been a visual feast if they had. Wood had positioned himself well within everyone's sightline and scribbled in a notepad he was carrying. He looked at a renter's face, and wrote. Looked and wrote. *Everyone* watched Wood.

Mr. Feldstein retook the stage. "A landlord is obligated, morally obligated, to provide heat, hot water, and reasonable privacy to his tenants." The crowd turned its attention back to the ancient man. "I did a disservice to all of you by selling to this... man. I did not fulfill my moral obligation to

you. But I am an old man, and sick. I cannot undo
the wrong. I cannot give you what Mr. Wood has
withheld." As Mr. Feldstein's voice rose, so did the
pack courage. Several disgruntled residents glared
outright at Wood and his determined scribbling.
"But, I can give you advice. And it will be *good* advice." There was a smattering of shy applause. "And
to prove I'm not just some old *schmuck* who's all
talk, I am also donating a check for one thousand
dollars to the association fund to be used toward legal costs."

Damned if Mr. Feldstein didn't bring down the
house. He dropped the check in front of Michelle.
"And, darling," he said to her, "you'd better open
that escrow account." Turning again to the tenants,
he waved, picked up his coat, and said, "I'm an old
man. If you will all excuse me, I'm going to go home
now. I have a pressing date with Murphy Brown."

"SHE'LL STEAL IT!" screamed the ubiquitous
Lucy, pointing directly at me—or perhaps it was the
dart board. An unbidden flashback to the death
grimace on the face of Mr. Hillerman, lying on the
floor, swept over me. I shuddered, trying to shake the
image. Mr. Feldstein gave me a sympathetic shrug
and tottered his exit.

Lucy bellowed again, "It's not the landlord who's
giving us trouble. It's BOWERING!" The assembly
started shifting in their seats, a little bored in antici-
pation of more fluoride talk. Or perhaps they were
beginning to believe their own stoop chatter; that I'd

made one too many trips down a Korean market aisle, and found a way to put a permanent stop to Mr. Hillerman's appetite for fresh fruits and vegetables.

Lucy was just warming up, however. "Get that check away from her. Quick. Somebody grab it! Don't lower your eyes at me; you know what I'm saying is true. Everyone knows it. I'm warning you. Don't you CARE, you worms? Bowering is going to take our money and get LIPOSUCTION."

Liposuction? Really. A little nose bob, perhaps, but *liposuction?* My birthday wasn't for another SEVEN DAYS. Ivan, in professional bartender mode, took Lucy by the arm and led her away. He smirked at me and comforted the resident nutburger with, "Let me buy you a drink, Lucy. At the Hi-Life. Right down the street, where they have bottled water."

Omar Salim turned around in his chair and nodded approval to Ivan, who saluted smartly. So, I thought, Ivan's no 1960s draft dodger. Unbidden, flashes of posttraumatic stress disorder passed through my brain as we all watched Lucy and Ivan leave.

The audience went wild. Wood smugged it out.

Not that I felt particularly powerful—lumpy around the thighs maybe—fading Vietcong imaginings flitting through my consciousness, but I retook control anyway.

What the hell. It was my paranoia, might as well make good use of it.

"I would like to take this opportunity to move that we discuss using our windfall to retain the services of a good landlord/tenant law firm. There is the matter of illegal MCIs to be pursued." My upstairs neighbor, the writer, seconded. The ayes had it.

"Big, fuckin' deal," Wood singsonged. "BIG fuckin' deal. You think I haven't won against better pissy groups than this? You can give me a pain in the ass, but you can't win. Take my advice and go home to the apartments you live in because *I say* you can live in 'em. Use the petty cash to buy some tree guards." The murmuring convinced me the barroom bravery was pissing away from my compatriots, along with the beer they'd tossed back during the meeting.

"You shit," I said from behind my teeth. Barry sat, lawyerly, without saying a word, probably wondering how his appointment could have canceled and left him in such a distasteful position. That would be vertical, I silently sniped.

Maybe she had to wash her straight brown hair.

"If I may have the floor," Omar addressed me. I nodded, since I didn't have a gun and all. "Mr. Wood, I believe it is, may I ask what your investment is in these buildings?"

"What, you got a calculator with you?"

Omar did not sink to Wood's below-sea-level. "I have taken the liberty to inquire as to the tax assessments, as well as the reasonable selling price of comparable facilities within this neighborhood. From this, I have calculated the approximate value of your properties over which we are now quibbling.'' Omar wrote a figure on a piece of paper, and showed it to Wood. ''Correct?'' Wood's face lost its sickly color and went directly to pasty. Do not pass go, do not collect two hundred dollars. ''Mr. Wood, you have owned these properties for slightly over one year. I have on record the price you paid, which was sixteen and one-half percent less than the figure I just showed you. I am prepared to offer you twenty percent above that number, if you will turn the real estate over to my holding company within the next thirty days.''

The audience was spellbound. Omar had them in the palm of his hand. He was knocking 'em dead. He was BOFFO. Who *was* this man? And while I was pondering that, where the hell did he come from?

Wood took the paper with Omar's figure and crushed it into a small, hard wad. He spit, twice if memory serves me, and lobbed it directly at the dart board (me).

Wood looked at me. ''Trust me, the slut's not worth it.''

''I'll call your office in the morning,'' Omar replied, unruffled.

I'll admit it. I was ruffled, big time. Barry was impassive. I questioned why being married to him had made me feel so safe. It was a start on the road to recovery, I hoped.

"Fuckin' camel jockey," Wood spit again and huffed out of the meeting. There was tumultuous applause from the regulars at the far end of the bar in objective appreciation of a fine performance.

I called for a motion to adjourn the meeting, which the British barmaid seconded even though she didn't have the right, and the ayes had it. I picked up the dangling phone, said goodbye to Jewel—who was laughing her copious ass off—and hung up. I really needed a drink, and the answer to a few questions. Omar first. I don't like to look a gift white knight in the visor, but—

Timmy, cute, familiar, and married, had come on duty behind the bar and slid a Wild Turkey bourbon—on the rocks, water-back— in front of me. The look on my face was obviously clearer than any spoken request. I took a long swig as the petrified forest of males encased me again. Omar dropped three one-hundred-dollar bills on the bar, and told Timmy to buy a round for the house. I was too rattled to be impressed that Omar then made the effort to promise to call me the next day, and left like the gentleman I was beginning to believe he was. Salim's exit was so brisk, clean, and smooth as to be, well, professional.

Brad tossed back his martini and gestured for another. Barry asked for a Guinness.

"I like him," Barry offered, his opinion uninvited.

"Who?" Brad asked.

"The Arab. Omar Salim." Barry nodded toward the door Omar had just exited. "Can't last, though."

"Cultural differences," Brad concurred. I polished off the bourbon. Timmy free-poured another.

"Nice guy, though," Barry said.

"Seems it," Brad agreed. "Rich as Croesus. Saw a file on him just a few weeks ago for some special on the continuum of Mideast economics relative to political upheaval."

How did I meet him?

"M.I.T. graduate," Barry added. "No wonder he has money."

Susie introduced us.

"No kidding," Brad commented. "Dartmouth, myself."

Susie?

"No kidding," Barry countered. "I'm U of Wisconsin, Madison, myself. No ivy, but a great party campus."

Male bonding is a terrifying thing to witness, especially when a woman is trying to think. My life had gone from the pits to euphoria back to as-yet unmined depths of new pits, and two of my ex-lovers were making fraternity small talk. Next thing, they'd be talking football.

Barry checked out the TV mounted over the door. "Who's playing?"

"Buffalo against the Redskins," Brad answered, eyes glued to the set.

"Excuse me," I interrupted. Neither man acknowledged me. "Pardon me, Barry, but unless I missed something obvious, I am in the deep shit with my landlord at this very moment."

"Not to mention the scuttlebutt about the Riveras and Hillerman," Barry nodded agreement. The Bills scored and my two pillars of strength let out a yelp of encouragement.

"Barry!"

"What? I'm listening."

"What am I going to do? Forget the stupid gossip. Wood came by this afternoon and threatened me. He said he wouldn't approve any sublet I applied for."

"That's illegal, Vic. Wood cannot unreasonably withhold approval of a sublet." Barry shouted again at the television, just as though the teams could hear him. "What do you mean, 'threatened'?"

"He implied that if I were 'nice' to him, my problems would stop," I enlightened my companions. The implications were lost when the Redskins regained control of the ball.

"What?" Barry and Brad asked at the same time with approximately the same measure of indifference.

"Wood as much as told me he'd make nice if I had sex with him."

"Makes sense to me," Ivan said from behind me. I looked around to see if Loony Lucy had appeared with him. He took the beer Timmy handed him, and shook his head. "I left your buddy Lucy at the Hi-Life. Wow. She really *hates* you." Ivan shrugged and swallowed beer directly from the bottle. "And I thought you looked so innocuous."

Innocuous?

"Where'd you go to college, Ivan?" Barry asked via some hidden agenda that I, as mere woman, could not fathom.

"Naval Academy, Class of Seventy," Ivan tossed away over the lip of the pale green bottle, as Barry blanched to about the same shade. "Then Georgetown," he said and sucked down the rest of his beer, gesturing for another round at the same time.

Brad, being an Ivy guy himself, was undaunted. "Hey, then maybe you know—"

I kicked the bar hard enough to startle any patron within a foot of contact with the wood. The three men circling me looked at me as though surprised I was still there.

"Well, thank you all, you big, strong he-men, so *very* much for your help. I can't tell you how much your educated advice and counsel has meant to me. I will cherish the memory of this moment every second I spend standing—dressed in ill-fitting K mart clothing—in the local soup kitchen lines."

Barry's attitude adjusted.

"This is really getting to you, isn't it?" he asked with all the intuitiveness I'd come to expect from an ex-whatever. He lowered his voice. Wouldn't want to cause a *scene*, would we? "Vic, you're going to have to get some control here. It's not good for you to allow yourself to get so upset."

"No," I answered, "I am actually not even close to upset. This afternoon I was upset. *Now* I'm verging on hysteria." Brad and Barry watched with concern. Ivan observed dispassionately—which was, at least, probably an honest emotion. "I'm not the bad guy here. What does Wood have to do to me before I'm allowed to defend myself? The man is *ruining* my life. He has implied to the police that I had an interest in killing Mr. Hillerman, and people are beginning to look at me really funny." The men quietly monitored me for the first signs of blatant mouth-frothing. "Why won't anybody but Slasher listen to me?"

Oh-oh. Self-pity was crawling into my voice. I try to save that for last-ditch efforts. Ivan was not yet inured, and patted my back. Still, it was the sort of pat one gives a dog for an especially fine roll over and play dead.

"Look," Barry said, "it so happens that Wood's son is an attorney. I know him socially. Let me give him a call first thing tomorrow morning and see what I can do. Would that be a help?" Since I was afraid I was going to start to cry again, I put on my I-am-woman, hear-me-roar look, and tried to listen the way I thought Margaret Thatcher would. "And you ought to report Wood's behavior as sexual harassment to the police yourself, okay? But, most of all, I think you ought to call someone to talk to. Someone who can, well, help you deal with your anger."

Brad nodded agreement.

"Toward whom?" asked Ivan. I was impressed that he knew to use 'whom'; Iron Maggie would have. I was clutching at straws, a little afraid the guys were right.

"That's why she should see someone," said Barry, "to work that out. In the meantime, if you're worried about your safety, what about Duchinski?"

Why do I feel obligated to answer questions like that? "Sergeant Duchinski and I are"—what were the words I wanted?—"no longer an item." Those weren't the words. Those were Deborah Kerr's words. Oh, well.

"Really?" responded my a capella trio in unison.

I was suddenly extremely fatigued. I found Michelle and Fran in the crowd and the three-girls-three political action committee trudged our manless way home.

For once, that suited me just fine.

As Margaret Thatcher said when saying her farewells to the House of Commons, "It's a funny old world."

Of course, she had Dennis.

EIGHT

Thursday, October 25

BLUBLUBLUB. BLUBLUBLUB. I thought I heard my frog telephone burble at me, but I was up to my armpits in paper and economic projections. Barry was right on the money, so to speak. It was sublet, or die. I was also a wee bit hung over, so I had earplugs in as a defense against the dynamic Julio and Company. When the answering machine picked up, I unstoppered one ear and pressed it to the speaker.

"BEEP. This is Mike, your stage manager speaking. We need your Mame contracts signed and back to us ASAP. This is, uh, the twenty-fifth. If we don't have the paperwork by the thirtieth, there's going to be one happy understudy wearing your costumes. You have the number. ASAP."

I replugged. The papers spread on the coffee table in front of me sneered. Numbers don't lie, and the ones I was looking at weren't even being kind. I did two sets: one for if I stayed in the city unemployed; the other for leaving town without subletting. It was a clear choice: starvation or starvation. Not to mention Slasher. I called everyone I'd ever known—even my parents—and no one would take him.

I considered smuggling the cat in my luggage.

He'd smother en route.

I considered paying Carlotta to move into my apartment. Paying with what?

I considered having a cheap, lurid physical encounter with Harvey Wood.

I took a cold bath and reconsidered.

I was used to having limited choices, but this no-way-out business was causing my brain to lock up like a transmission that had been double-clutched one too many times. I paced. I redid the numbers and paced some more. I stared at the blipping light on my answering machine and wondered how long I could stall the producers. And then I paced some more.

BLAHHHHHHHHHHHHHHHHHHHHHHHHHT. The infamous Wood buzzer howled at me. There is no sound deafener on the market today that can blank that blast when trapped in the same room. I was at the door anyway, so I looked out the peep hole to see who wanted a shot at me. If it was Wood, I was going to call the cops.

BLAHHHHHHHHHHHT. It was the cops.

It was Dan. BLAHHHHHHHHHHHT. I checked my reflection in the mirror by the door, my heart thudding like a jackhammer. Amazingly, my face didn't appear nearly as ugly as my prospects. BLAHHHHH-HHHT. I foofed my hair and buzzed the door open, swiping cat hairs from my chest so that I wouldn't leave a tacky hug imprint. Everything was going to be all right.

My cheeks flushed with pleasure—a good thing since I hadn't put on any makeup. Wouldn't want Dan to take one look at death-warmed-over and change his mind again. I simply needed him too desperately. Slasher recognized Dan's heavy tread down the hall and bounced to the door to wait for a little roughing up. Boys are so cute when they play, don't you think? I planted a demure, yet delighted, smile on my face and opened the door.

"Dan," I said. Very Julia Roberts.

"Hi, Vic," Dan said, bending to pick up Slasher. Very Lorne Greene. Uh-oh. Dan nuzzled the cat as he stood in the doorway. "Miss me, boy? Yes. That's a *good* boy. *What* a fine boy." Slasher inclined his head and tentatively encased the tip of Dan's nose with his mouth, then licked it twice to prove he didn't mean anything hostile. I reached up and stroked the big cop's cheek to prove that *I* didn't plan to be hostile, either. Hell, I was prepared to be downright groveling. A commiseration on a massive chest was just what the doctor ordered. Then I could ask Dan to take Slasher. That would solve *one* problem, at least.

"Wish I could take you, Slash," Dan murmured into the cat pelt, one step ahead of me, as usual. "But no pets allowed in my building." He put the cat down on the carpet. Slasher flung himself on his back with a thunk for some manly scratching, but Dan stood rigid at the door.

So he needed some encouragement. Fine. Terrific by me. No problem. I placed both hands on Dan's broad chest and ran them slowly up to around his neck, pressed my body against his, and drank in the comforting scent of maleness and Old Spice. And—unless Dan had taken to carrying a contraband firearm—he was pleased to see me, too.

"I missed you, Dan," I whispered into his neck. He hadn't shaved that morning. I love that.

"No, Vic." He disentangled my arms from around his neck.

Okay. No groping. I could do that. For a while. They always cave in eventually; Gramma told me so. The door closed behind Dan, at last.

"Can I get you something? Is it too early for a beer, or would you like a cup of coffee? It's all ready."

"I'm on duty, Vic."

Okay. Scratch the beer. I started toward the kitchen to get the coffee, "Just milk, right?"

"I can't stay, Vic." Dan pulled in a deep breath and stayed rooted to his security guard position. "I only came by to let you know that there has been a complaint lodged against you at the Twentieth Precinct. A friend called me to let me know. I figured you'd rather hear it from me than from a white shield."

"What?" was my brilliant comeback.

"It's been alleged that you've made some threatening telephone calls" was Dan's. He was watching me carefully, ever the cop. "That's a federal rap, Vic."

I was speechless. Even Deborah Kerr was without words.

Dan continued, "You don't have to tell me, Vic, but did you do it?"

"NO. No, I did *not* do it. And who am I supposed to have threatened, anyway? Like I'm such a big worry to the community at large." I felt as though I were going to be ill. Partly because of the accusation, partly because Dan thought I might be guilty. "Was it Loony Lucy? Because if it was, let me tell you, I have a few suspicions about the Lucrezia Borgia of West Eightieth Street, myself." WHAM. Another flash of Mr. Hillerman dead on the floor. "My, God," Maybe I wasn't the only make-believe sister doing the old man's shopping.

"Your landlord." Dan checked a notepad. "Harvey Wood. He called it in first thing this morning. Said you called late last night and then twice again this morning."

"Well, I didn't," I said while flipping around the sickening possibilities of Lucy expanding her pharmaceutical horizons with human subjects.

"Will you listen to what I'm saying here? This is serious."

"Only if I did it, Duchinski."

"I'm just letting you know what he reported, Vic."

"Oh, sure. Look at your face. Part of you *believes* it. How *could* you?"

"Look, Vic. You've been under a lot of pressure lately. Everyone knows it. You've been acting strange, even for you." Dan was sounding like my mother. He even looked like my mother at that moment: long-suffering. "He told the desk sergeant about refusing your sublet. I know what that theater tour means to you, babe, and I'm sorry. But you can't go around trying to intimidate people." Tears burbled up in my eyes. Dan crumbled and took me in his arms. "Nobody knows that better than I do."

It felt so good to just lean.

Dan continued. "It gets worse, Vic."

"I've heard *that* before."

"The Twentieth is investigating Sam Hillerman's death. They're looking into that Rivera woman's accident, too. There have been some, uh, accusations."

I pushed the man from whom I had wanted nothing more than a hug two minutes before away from me. "I *didn't* do it. Do you seriously think that I don't know paid professionals who could do the job better than me? Why, in God's name, would I put myself in deeper ca-ca than I'm already in?"

"I don't know, Vic. It doesn't make any sense. But you haven't been behaving very rationally lately, now have you? I just thought I'd try to help."

"Thank you so very much," said Deborah Kerr. Vic Bowering added, "You son-of-a-bitch. I can get that kind of help just about anywhere in New York, from total strangers."

Dan looked at me. His expression told me I'd just confirmed his suspicions, and that it didn't give him any particular thrill to be right. Obviously, this was not an auspicious moment to start ranting about Lucy's psychotic behavior and personal motivation for bumping off the elderly occupant of a two-bedroom rent-stabilized apartment.

I believe I may have shrieked at Dan to get out, but I'd rather block that memory. I wanted him gone, but he planted himself at the door.

"One more thing, Vic, and then I'll go. Your neighbor Tom Daily, next building down, was killed last night. Gunshot to the head. It looks like suicide, but his apartment was ransacked, so we can't rule out homicide. Since the blue boys are already sniffing around, well, it could get difficult. Keep your nose clean, your security grate secured, and don't buzz anyone you don't know into the building. Okay?"

It was not okay. Not okay at all, but I was too hurt to admit I was frightened. But then, everyone has one of those years, and I was not about to get "help." Not from Dan, not from anybody.

Whether I needed help or not, Dan left quietly. Again.

Slasher glared at me accusingly. His buddy had left and it was ALL MY FAULT.

There were no iron guardrails around the new honey locust trees and that was my fault. The trees were the wrong variety and that was my fault. I was poor and unemployed and that *certainly* was my fault. Jewel LaFleur was about to be evicted, and while that was not entirely my fault, I had definitely made the situation worse. Which was completely MY FAULT. Tom Daily was dead. If I'd organized a neighborhood patrol, would he still be walking his cocker spaniel around the block? Mr. Hillerman may have been poisoned because I was pretending not to be home instead of behaving like a decent human being. No doubt someone would inform me of my culpability for the Serbo-Croatian insurrection when I least expected it. Not that anyone needed to. I had myself for that.

Rather than plummet the remaining two and a half inches to the depths of total masochistic despair, I called Barry and demanded that he get his skinny butt immediately over to Jewel's apartment for some remedial work.

If I was going to get all the blame, I might as damned well do something to merit it.

NINE

Later

I MADE COFFEE while Jewel watched Australian rules football, the volume cranked up high enough to match her shouts of encouragement to some chap named Brian who, according to Jewel, sported the best set of buns in the league. During a lull, the buzzer went off. Through profuse intercom static, I recognized Barry's voice and hit the button to release the lobby door. Seven more buzzes convinced me the door wasn't operating again, so I went down the two flights to let my ex-husband into the building.

"I don't have time for this, Vic," Barry brushed past me and up the stairs. "I have appointments. I *work*." He had to wait at Jewel's door until I found the keys. I started to feel guilty. I repressed it. Brian Buns scored as Barry and I crossed the threshold.

"YESSSSSS!" Jewel cheered.

I punched the mute button on the remote control and asked who wanted coffee. Barry said his stomach was acting up. Jewel told me to turn the TV back on. I told her, very firmly, that she could watch it without sound. Very Margaret Thatcher. My friend and ex looked at one another, perplexed and quiet, while I got my own damned coffee.

"All right," I said, "we are in a situation here, and I would like to do what needs to be done before I go completely out of my gourd. Or," I amended, "out of town. Whichever comes first, and it's a horse race." The Odd Couple humored me. "First, Barry, did you have a chance to talk with Wood's son?"

"I said I would, didn't I?"

"Yes, but did you?"

"I did." Barry was sulking. He wasn't used to my being efficient.

"And?"

"And, he doesn't know anything about the landlord business. He never liked it and never involved himself in any aspect of it."

"I believe," Jewel offered, "I heard the same spiel during World War Two from an entire nation."

"Then why is he listed on the incorporation papers for Wood's holding company as president?" I asked.

Barry looked annoyed. My guess is that he *was* annoyed. "A formality," he answered. "Most privately held corporations list relatives as officers. It doesn't mean they have anything to do with the operation of the business."

"Terrific," I grumped.

"Look," Barry interrupted, "Dave Wood is a nice guy. It's not his fault that his father's a slime. You wanted me to ask; I asked. Dave remembers you from the New York Bar Association *Messiah* sing-along a couple of years ago, Vic. He even said your rendition of 'He Was Despised' brought tears to his eyes. But his hands are tied. We're talking family, Vic."

"Okay, okay," I muttered. Jewel's hand was creeping toward the remote control. I snatched it away before she could turn up the volume. "Now where exactly are you, Jewel, with Wood?"

She leaned nearer the TV screen. Brian Buns scored again. "YESSSSS!" Jewel sat back into the cushions. "What, darling?"

I repeated the question, hoping divine patience would guarantee me some kind of heavenly Emmy.

Jewel waved a hand at the carved Gothic side-board next to me. "The eviction notices are in there somewhere."

Barry's jaw dropped. "You mean you've been served with eviction more than *once?*" I pulled open the long drawer and located the legal papers.

"Twice," Jewel confirmed, grabbing the remote control and goosing up the volume. I grabbed it back and shut off everything.

"What does that mean in terms of time?" I asked Barry.

"Three months, tops. Jeez, Jewel, why didn't you show these to someone?" Barry asked, taking the papers from my hand and reading quickly. "We should have taken some action immediately."

"We?"

I tried to reason. "Jewel, I'm going to be out of town when the shit hits the fan; so is Fran. Michelle has a real job and won't have the kind of time it takes to cover your butt."

"Champagne, anyone?" Jewel asked pleasantly.

"Jewel! This is not the time to be drinking."

"On the contrary. I can't think of a better time. Barry, would you be a dear and pour me a glass of whatever's open in there?"

Barry has always left cases of temporary insanity to me, feeling that I am best equipped to deal with them, so he went to the kitchen, shaking his head.

"Vic," she said, taking my hand, "I have managed to survive for over seventy years without your protection. It's lovely to have you offer it, of course"—she accepted a glass of champagne from Barry—"but I don't require it. Everything always works out for the best." She sipped. "And that in a nutshell is why you have stomach problems and I do not."

Barry slapped his thighs and hefted his briefcase. "She's right, Vic. I think you have enough problems of your own right now. Serious problems. So, if you'll excuse me, Jewel, I have a meeting on the East Side I have to get to." Jewel smiled placidly and toasted him. "Vic, why don't you walk me down?"

"Go, sweetheart, we'll talk later," Jewel instructed. She took possession of the remote control and flicked the picture back on. She was immedi-

ately riveted by toned men in short shorts. The roar
of the crowd was my cue to exit.

"I'm going to stop Wood, Jewel, anyway I can,"
I promised and padded after Barry down the stairs.
"What happens if I sublet without Wood's ap-
proval? Can he evict me right away?"

"Of course not. This *is* New York."

"Great!"

"It'll take three months to go through all the motions."

"But I'll be in, uh, I don't know, somewhere that
isn't here in three months."

"Exactly." Barry held the door for me and then
bolted toward Amsterdam Avenue. I chased after.

"Then I can't get away with it?"

"Sure you can," Barry affirmed, "for three
months. Then you're out on your ass." We crossed
the street so Barry could hail a cab heading cross-
town on Eighty-first Street. "Besides, Vic, you've
never gotten away with anything in your life. Everyone knows that."

"You mean, he's *got* me, just like that?"

Barry raised his hand, and a medallion cab nearly
ran me over to get to him. He pulled open the car
door, kissed me on the mouth like Ward Cleaver
saying bye-bye to June, and sagely quoted, "Never
confuse justice with the law, Vic." The cab cut off
the M-79 bus and took the corner eastbound on three
wheels. Over the screech of brakes, I heard tapping

behind me. Ivan beckoned from behind the plate-glass window of McAleer's.

So did Mr. Jack Daniels.

Double-checking that the sun was, indeed, over the yardarm, I joined Jack and Ivan and Genny. I hadn't even gotten to the part of my personal soap opera that included the Loony Lucy and threatening phone calls scenarios. Might as well repress.

Ivan regarded me curiously. You'd think he'd never seen a reasonably well-bred thirty-nine-ish woman tossing back boilermakers. He made the mistake of asking me what was wrong. I made the mistake of not abbreviating the tale of woe to end right along with the first bourbon.

"Are you telling me," Ivan asked, "that the offer of a sublet is out?"

"NO," I refused to surrender, "there's a way. I just haven't figured it out yet. There's always a way. I have four whole days to think of something."

"Like what?"

"I don't know. Anything can happen in four days. God made the world in six, some dinkoid landlord/tenant thing in an inconsequential pimple on the ass of Manhattan shouldn't take more than two-thirds the time of creation."

Having said that, I wondered about the expression "In a New York Minute." I threw down the dregs of my whiskey, and Ivan repoured. If a New York Minute is so damned short, why are the Motor Vehicle lines so damned LONG? Why are New Yorkers always so LATE? And why doesn't the mail or the subway ever COME?

Ivan's voice cut through the philosophical haze.

"There are guys who take care of problems like yours."

"Thanks. I've had a lawyer." Since I set myself up, I paid it off. "More than once."

"That's not what I meant," Ivan corrected. "There are—persons."

Oh, I got it. "Mob?"

Ivan sighed over my naïveté. "Not always."

So, I didn't *quite* get it. Don't you hate it when men get cryptic on you? Well, I do, especially when I'm drinking on an empty stomach.

"Arms or legs are not good enough for me anymore, Ivan. This is war, and I don't come from such highly evolved stock myself." I threw down a twenty on the bar. "I am a registered Republican in New York City. I don't know the meaning of the word 'futility'!"

Ivan pushed the twenty back at me with a head shake reserved by bartenders just for tipsy women. "Salim seems to be on your side. Maybe you should sit back and wait. Just think about it."

"Yeah, yeah," I muttered, gratefully returning the twenty to my wallet and dropping a fiver, "except sometimes I think I'm the only person in New York with a time schedule." In my position, every little economy counts. "Look how far waiting and thinking has gotten me. And as for depending on a man to bail me out, no thanks. If it actually worked, I'd consider it."

"You going to be all right?" Ivan asked as I got up to leave.

"Oh, fine. I'm always fine." I leaned over the bar and kissed him fondly, like an old husband. Booze does that to me, but at least it doesn't make me dance on bars or punch out blondes.

In an inspired moment of boozy irony, I fed a buck into the jukebox and punched the code to play "Someone to Watch Over Me" four times before I carefully marched out.

Maybe it was a national petty criminal holiday, because I got back into my apartment without incident, despite my incapacitation. I fell over my own shoes in the living room, but at least landed on the sofa. This was not skill. The apartment is too small to fall down anywhere uncaught.

Slasher wandered out from the bedroom, sat in front of me, and stared as though he expected me to do something for him, so I turned on the TV and fell asleep.

Brad Sinclair's voice woke me during the eleven o'clock news. I watched without enthusiasm through his sign-off, "That's the Big Apple on Thursday, October twenty-fifth." Since I hate falling asleep before a room has ceased to carousel, I picked up the *TV Guide* to find out what followed good old Brad on the tube. My eyes weren't focusing as well as they ought, so it was a three- or four-second delay before I realized I'd gone blind.

De facto, anyway. The power had gone off, leaving the entire building in blackness.

Stumbling to the alley window, I reassured myself the power failure wasn't citywide, so the probability of being overrun with crazed looters was only marginally higher than any other weeknight.

Good New Yorker that I am, I said the hell with everything, and tripped off to bed and sleep.

TEN

Friday, October 26

BLAHHHHHHHHHHHHHHHHHHHHHHHHHHHHHT.   I
slammed the Off switch on my flamingo alarm clock.
BLAHHHHHHHT. BLAHHHHHHHHHHHHHHHHT.

So, it wasn't the alarm. I opened my eyes and
stared blindly at the clock dial, raising my eyebrows
valiantly and hoping that would somehow restore my
sight. BLAHHHHHHHHHHHHT.

It didn't, so I turned on the bedside lamp. I could
see; it was a MIRACLE. The clock read six-fifty. In the
morning? I reached for the TV remote, dropped it
twice, and turned on the television. Courtesy of Fox
Channel Five early news, I grasped the ugly truth. It
was, indeed, the morning after. My head rang like a
gong with the beginnings of what would undoubt-
edly evolve into one of the world's champion hang-
overs. Since the intercom had stopped stabbing me,
I turned off the TV and rolled over for the fifteen
minutes I knew I'd have before Julio and the boys
arrived for breakfast. I figured I could hate the guts
of whatever moron would buzz me before noon after I'd had some aspirin.

I heard my front door open, along with the clatter
of hundreds of keys. Slasher—great guard cat that he

is—scrambled from beneath the covers, leaving skid marks up the length of my right leg, to check out our unexpected company. Slasher loves guests. I was in my underwear and feeling less hospitable. Not to mention stupid.

Try as I might, I couldn't remember where I'd put the Mace my father had given me for Christmas. As far as I could remember, all actresses found bludgeoned to death in their beds are found inelegantly clad in their undies. Perfect. To top it all off, an ignominious end.

"Meezfik!"

So much for the dramatic.

It was Carlotta, who had let herself into my apartment at, I checked, 6:53 A.M. I pulled my silk kimono from a pile of clothing next to the bed, hung it on my decrepit body, and slowly felt my way to the living room, turning on lights as I went.

Imagine my surprise.

Flanking Carlotta were two plainsclothes detectives. How did I know their profession upon first sight? I don't know. How is it that people spot evangelical ministers and insurance salesmen? It's some subliminal survival thing.

"What's the matter?" I asked, wishing I hadn't lost the sash to my robe.

"Oh, Meezfik!" Carlotta wailed and threw herself into my arms.

I did the right thing and held the sobbing super, all the while wishing I'd worn my formal underwear, since it was now showing.

Fortunately, as an actress, I'm not really modest. I have this "faux modesty" that I do for the benefit of my mother and society in general, but one stint dressing backstage in a musical gets a woman over shame at her nakedness in about forty-seven seconds. The younger, skinny cop blushed. I sat Carlotta on the sofa, and wondered if anyone had ever actually died of a hangover.

"Let me make some coffee," I offered, more for myself than the suffering Carlotta.

"Sure," agreed the Grizzly Adams cop, studiously not noticing my disarray.

"Chu haf Courvoisier?" Carlotta asked benignly. My stomach did a quick flip at the mere mention.

"Bourbon, peach schnapps, or soy sauce," I answered, piling unmeasured coffee into my machine. It crossed my mind that I wasn't actually awake, just having a surreal sort of nightmare.

"Burpins hokee," Carlotta made her choice. Too bad for me that "burpin" was so very "hokee" for me the night before. When I pulled the stopper from the bottle of Maker's Mark, the fumes nearly toppled me. I went into the bathroom and brushed my teeth, then hung over the bathroom sink for a while before daring to return to pour a healthy shot into a brandy snifter. I held it away from my nose to get it into Carlotta's hand.

"Rough night?" asked the nonblushing man.

"Not at all," Deborah Kerr answered for me. "Coffee, gentlemen?" I pulled the carafe out to get a mug of brew before it was ready. I added tap water and slugged down the entire cup, listening to the sizzle of the dripped water on the heating element.

The men both said no thanks, and I poured a second undiluted measure for myself.

"What's going on?" I asked from the bedroom. The sash had disappeared, so I put on an elastic belt from the top of the pile and brought my coffee back to the living room.

Carlotta let loose with a lengthy explanatory paragraph of some language I can only assume is classical Romanian. I sat on the arm of the sofa, patted her shoulder, and directed my attention to the Bobbsey Twins From Hell.

"Who are you?"

"I'm Detective Franklin, and this is Sawicki," the big guy answered, flipping open his identification and gold shield case. Sure enough. He was Franklin. "May I ask your whereabouts last night around eleven to midnight?"

"I was here."

Carlotta held out her empty glass. I took it for a refill and noted the dubious look from both men.

"Alone?" asked the previously retiring Sawicki.

"Yes, alone." I put the glass back on the coffee table, becoming more and more irritated. "What's this all about? Did someone accuse me of stockpiling nuclear weapons? Chemical warfare? Bestiality?"

Franklin sat in the Lincoln rocker. Sawicki picked up Slasher and rubbed his ears.

"A man was murdered in this building last night, Ms. Bowering. We're interviewing residents to find out if anyone heard or saw anything unusual," Franklin explained, picking cat hairs from his dark blue overcoat.

When will I learn to keep my wit banked?

"Who?"

"Your landlord, Harvey Wood."

I tried very hard not to look relieved, which I was, even in my condition. It's not that I'd lost sight of the importance of a police chat, but there is a certain comfort in finding out that the victim was pig slime. There was a male dancer with a strong preference for S&M bars living on the fifth floor of whom I was rather fond. Were I a betting woman, my money would have been on him for the homicide lotto, so Wood's hitting God's big Pick 6 allayed one of my fears.

"Last night?" I asked stupidly.

"Yeah. Your superintendent, Ms.—," Franklin double-checked his notes, "—Domincescu found his body at approximately five-ten this morning when she went to take a look at the main breaker board in the basement.''

"Ah," I said before I thought about it. "That's why the lights went out."

"We think so, yes," Sawicki answered.

"What would old Harve have—," I began, when I couldn't resist a game show guess. "—No, don't tell me. He was diddling with the hot-water heater."

"The thermostat, actually, as far as we can tell. There was a short circuit of some kind, and Wood was electrocuted."

"Which shorted out the whole building," I finished.

"Exactly," Franklin said. "You seem to know something about electricity."

"Not really," I demurred. "My sister's the expert. Our father's an electrical engineer. I just picked up the jargon."

"You're an actress, right?" Franklin asked.

"Does it show?"

"No. Your neighbors said you are. Are you?"

"Yes. When I'm lucky."

Carlotta was holding up her glass again, hopefully. I took it from her and went to the kitchen to pour her another shot. Who said I can't take direction?

I heard Franklin raise his voice to carry, "And you were home all evening and neither saw nor heard anything out of order?" The smell of bourbon made me gag.

"That's right," I handed Carlotta the fresh snifterful. "No, wait a minute. I was out until, oh, I don't know when. I went to McAleer's for a drink, came back here and fell asleep. It was early, though, before ten o'clock, I guess."

"I see," Franklin muttered in a way that worried me. "Well, that'll do for now, Ms. Bowering." He rose from the rocking chair; Sawicki put Slasher down carefully on the end table. "If you don't mind, could I use your bathroom?"

"Mi john es su john."

Sawicki picked the cat back up as Franklin made his way past me and toward the bathroom. He paused in the kitchen.

"You got some messages on your machine."

"Thanks," I answered, uninterested. Then I remembered Mike the stage manager and my "real life." When the bathroom door closed, I went to the answering machine and hit Play.

"BEEP. Vic, this is Fran. Are you monitoring your calls? If you are, pick up because I want to talk to you. Vic? Come on, Vic? Vic, I'm really worried about you, I've never seen you so... oh, shit. Give me a call. CLICK."

"BEEP. Vic, this is Barry. Just wanted to know if you've calmed down. Since you're not there, I guess you have. Call me tomorrow at the office. CLICK."

"BEEP. Vic, dammit, this is Fran again at around ten o'clock. Call me when you get in. CLICK."

"BEEP. Vic, darling, this is Jewel, just checking up on you. Ben told me how upset you are. Hope you're having a wonderful time, no matter who you're doing. Ha! CLICK."

"Victoria, this is Omar Salim. Please accept my apologies for not calling you sooner, but I was unexpectedly called away on business. I will be leaving Tunis at my earliest opportunity and calling you upon my return. I sincerely hope that you are having no further problems and shall look forward to speaking with you."

"BEEP. All right, Vic, I give up. Call me tomorrow as soon as you can. It's past eleven and I need my beauty sleep . . . oh, this is Fran again. CLICK."

The toilet flushed. Franklin came into the kitchen, thanked me for the use of the facilities, and left with Sawicki. Carlotta threw down the dregs of her bourbon and left me with the glass. She seemed much, much more composed.

I took that opportunity to crawl back to bed, hoping the day would be long enough to sleep it off. I'd gloat later when my head wasn't pounding along with Julio upstairs. The super-duper wax earplugs came out of their travel case and went directly into my ear canals.

My grandmother always told me that there is no problem so great that, if you ignore it, it will not eventually go away.

Gramma, also, was so damned cute when she was being naive.

ELEVEN

Later

I WAS HAVING the loveliest dream. I dreamt I was in bed, stark naked, and big, old Dan Duchinski came into the room—very *Fear of Flying*—out of nowhere, saying nothing. He sat on the edge of my bed as I slept, and slid one of his magnificently muscled arms under the small of my back. I moved to accommodate, and made a small guttural noise at the back of my throat as he raised my shoulders from the warm bed sheets and crushed me to his chest.

It was so real, I could smell that stirring maleness. It was so real . . .

I opened my eyes.

Into Dan's chest. So close that my eyelashes were bent down. I hate that.

"Dan?"

Duchinski grabbed my arms and pushed me back onto the pillows. In the dim light I could see his lips moving, and the shadow of another person standing in the bedroom door. I couldn't make out the face. I sat up, shocked, and reached out to convince myself I was not dreaming. Some dream. Dan was in my bed wearing a ski parka, mouthing silently at me.

Terror. I was struck mute as well as deaf.

I remembered my ear plugs and pulled them out.

"—sus, Vic, you had us scared to death."

It was another MIRACLE. I could hear again. Dan's voice shouted on.

"Those things aren't safe, Vic. What if there'd been a fire? You'd never have heard the detector. Then I thought, my God, you might have *hurt* yourself." He slammed my head against his shoulder in a gesture of affection and concern that set up a conga jam-session in my hung-over brain, and held the back of my neck with his free hand. I thought I was going to faint from blood deprivation to the cerebrum, but Dan let go in time.

I squinted at the shadow in the doorway. It was Carlotta again. Was it last call already? "I'm fine," I asserted, not believing it.

"No, you're not," Duchinski grunted as he stood. "Carlotta, thanks for letting me in. You can go now." She shrugged and left the room. I heard the front door close behind her.

"Come to bed, Dan. We'll talk later, when I can."

"Get dressed, Vic. We're going to talk now." He threw my floor pile of clothes at me, to underscore his point. "I'll make you some coffee."

Struggling my arms into the kimono was beyond me, so I simply pulled a Three Mile Island souvenir T-shirt over my head, then tugged on some panties and socks. If ever Dan had the chance to get into bed with me without fear of my molesting him, this was it. I guess he blew it.

"Did you take a tranquilizer. A sleeping pill?" Dan demanded from the kitchen counter.

"No, I'm just not very good in the morning. You should have known that by now." I hugged him foggily from behind, leaning my head on his back, and starting to doze back off to sleep. He led me to the sofa and planted me like a radish. When the coffee was done, he wrapped my hand around a warm mug of it and sat next to me while I finished it. Then he brought me another.

"So, you were worried about me, huh?" I asked, watching him coquettishly over the rim of my Di and Charles cup.

"Are you awake now?"

"I'm moving."

"You were moving before. I asked if you're awake."

"What time is it?" I asked.

"Just after four."

"Then, no."

"Vic," Dan warned me.

"Yes, I'm awake."

"You're not dressed. And what happened to your hand? It looks like you stuck it in a Cuisinart."

He was right. The gashes on the palm of my right hand from my fearless attack on the garden wall were getting infected; I was just in too much peripheral pain to have noticed. I defended myself, "You didn't *ask* if I were dressed. You asked if I were—"

"They want you for questioning at the precinct, Vic. Sawicki called me to let me know. I said I'd bring you in myself."

"Why does everyone call you when my butt's in a sling? Is my phone number written on your bathroom wall or what?"

"This is serious, Vic." Dan pulled me up off the sofa and pushed me into the bedroom. I cringed when he turned on the overhead light, pushed his hand away from the switch, and substituted the boudoir lamp with the flattering pink bulb. Dan certainly looked serious enough. No need for me to look poorly lit.

"What do they want to talk to me about?" I pulled gray spandex dance pants and matching tunic from my drawer. Dan, ever the gentleman, turned his back to me. "I talked to a couple of cops this morning." I slung my TMI T-shirt to the floor and found a bra and pantyhose to put on. "I could really use some more sleep."

Dan turned to me, aghast. "What do you think they want to talk to you about? About Wood's murder. Jesus, Vic," he spoke directly into my Lily of France blush underwire, before he caught himself and turned back to the hallway. "Finish dressing, I'm going to call Laskin and have him meet us at the precinct house."

"Barry's number..." I started.

"Is on the autodial," Dan finished for me. "Above my number, as I recall."

I let Duchinski do his thing while I brushed my teeth a few more times and allowed myself a grimace in the bathroom mirror. My hair had become a living thing, untamed, bestial, so I threatened it up to the top of my head. Wild red tendrils escaped the elastic fencing, as I listened to the drone of Dan's voice from the other room. I washed my face, but my skin hurt too much to put on foundation. The mascara was enough to bring tears to my eyes. Or perhaps it was the cigarette I could neither get myself to actually smoke, nor put out.

Dan was holding my coat. "Can't you do something with your hair?" he asked. "You look like a hooker."

"I do not," though, of course, I did. "I'm not wearing makeup. What do you want from me?"

"Nothing." He threw the coat at me. "You still look like a hooker. Laskin's meeting us. We'll wait until he gets there."

"Fine. I don't care." I had to dig under the sofa for my purse. "Could we stop at the frozen yogurt place on the way? My stomach's a little funny."

Dan grabbed my arm and pulled me out the door and down the hall. We didn't speak during the walk to the precinct, but, en route, he did buy me a double-dip chocolate macadamia nut cone at Häagen Dazs. I really, really, needed some more sleep.

Obviously.

Dan didn't stick around for any questioning. Barry was waiting at the entrance to the Twentieth and took possession of my person as though I were a grocery bag, and hustled me into the lobby.

"Where'd Dan get to so fast?" I asked Barry.

"Work. Some people *do* work. He overstepped himself by going to get you, as it is. Now, come on, let's get this over with."

I sat like a nice girl in one of the khaki green molded plastic chairs set in the center of the twenty-foot square room and examined the decor. It was not the kind of place where one could drift off to sleep, anyway. The combination of orange, tan, beige, and dark brown ceramic tiles grappling with the electric blue walls made me realize exactly what decorating scheme could be produced if Burger King and Howard Johnson worked closely together. On acid.

Barry talked with the desk sergeant in that low, lawyer tone he's perfected. I smoked and read posters.

I learned not to do drugs, and that—though plenty tall enough—I was too old to sign up for the upcoming class at the police academy.

Barry sat with me for my questioning. I rather like extemporaneous speaking, but after an hour of not smoking in a tiny windowless room with Franklin, Sawicki, and Barry, I was bored spitless. Worse, I'm a quick study with remarkably rotten long-term memory. For some fuzz-reasons, the two cops seemed inordinately concerned with my where-abouts for several nights; and though the night before was relatively fresh, the other dates had dissipated into the ozone of my brain. It seemed to me that I would, nonetheless, have remembered killing Harvey Wood, so the lapses bothered me less than everyone else.

It was nothing but the same stupid questions over and over again. When they finally said I could go, I got my second wind.

And I wanted there to be nicotine in it.

I lit up on the entrance stairs. Barry sat on the top step and looked more like he was going to barf than I felt like I was.

"Shit," he said. He looked at my cigarette. "I thought you were trying to quit."

"Must have been someone else you've had sex with."

"I wouldn't be so flip, if I were you. You're up the creek, Vic. God."

"I told them what I did. What's the problem?"

"What's the *problem?* You were drinking bourbon last night, weren't you? Don't deny it, I can always tell.

"The problem is that a man you don't even deny you loathed got killed in the basement of your building. And he did it at a time for which you have absolutely no alibi, on an evening you were, admittedly *again*, drinking to excess and under an enormous amount of stress.

"And, although it's not proof, Sawicki and Franklin both heard messages on your answering machine that were left during the time that you *claim* you were in the apartment. Additionally, God help us, you *volunteer* that you have a working key to the area in which Wood was electrocuted."

Uh-oh.

"I volunteered that?"

"You did. Shit." Barry stood and dusted off his beautifully creased trousers, "And *then,* you not only placidly confess to hating the man's guts, but run the police through exactly *why* you have a motive to kill him."

"I did, didn't I?" I wished it were possible to efficiently smoke more than one cigarette at a time. I followed Barry down the path toward the sidewalk.

"Barry!" a man getting out of a cab called.

"Shit." Barry cursed under his breath. "It's Dave Wood, Harvey's son."

"Sorry to hear about your father, Dave," Barry told him.

"Thanks, Barry." Dave extended his hand to me. "Vic, right? We met at the *Messiah* sing-along a few years ago, didn't we?"

I couldn't remember, so I nodded a yes.

Dave Wood turned his attention back to my nearly-ex. "Barry, I'm glad I ran into you. Do you have time to come in here with me? A Detective Franklin called me in to ask a few questions, and I didn't have time to retain anyone to come with me."

"I thought you were a lawyer," I said to Dave.

"I am. I am. But, as Barry would tell you, any time you're being asked anything by the police, you should have counsel with you. It's just good practice, right Barry?''

"Sorry, Dave." Barry looked mortified. "I just got out. I'm representing Vic in this matter.''

"What?" Dave sputtered. "I don't believe it. Talk about the shotgun approach to investigation.''

"Do they even know your father's death was a homicide, or are they just spitting in the wind?'' Barry asked.

"Oh, it was murder, all right. The thermostat on the hot-water heater was tampered with—not professionally, but effectively enough. What would you know about anything like wiring, Vic?'' Dave patted my shoulder, and Barry gave me a look that shouted, in no uncertain terms, to keep my unbridled home-improvement mouth to myself. "Besides, it makes a lot more sense to suspect me than you, Vic, with all you have to lose.''

"How so?" Barry jumped in for me.

Dave Wood stammered. His face reddened. ''Well,'' he began haltingly, ''because of, uh, the arrangement.'' He looked at me pleadingly to save him. I couldn't, but I obviously didn't look particularly secretive, so Dave yammered on to Barry, "I mean, you two are *divorced,* and Vic's an attractive woman with a lot to offer a man. And Dad wasn't exactly repulsive himself, and—''

Barry glanced at me out of the sides of his eyes and assumed his in-total-control-of-the-situation pose.

I don't have one of those at my disposal. My
mouth dropped open as the light dawned.

Barry jerked my arm hard enough to hurt and
said, "We have to go, Dave. Again, sorry about your
father." He dragged me into traffic.

In the cab I protested, "I was not sleeping with
Wood, Barry. And, if I were, I'd be doing it in exchange for an apartment with sunlight *and* hot water."

"Oh? It would explain why you never made a sexual harassment complaint against him, wouldn't it?
And it's not like you've become a born-again virgin
during the year we've been separated, is it?" If my
hand weren't throbbing, I would have slapped his
face. "Cops, bartenders, TV news reporters, Lebanese real estate investors, Italian counts. I have to
hand it to you, your taste is eclectic."

"Here, cabdriver," I shouted through the Plexi-
glas security window, "Let me out, HERE." We
screeched to a halt, and I wrenched open the door.
"I'm not going to defend myself to you, Barry, a
man who would fuck a rock pile if he thought a
snake were *in it*." I slammed the door.

Great exit line, huh? Now the only free lawyer I
would ever have access to was pissed off at me.
Clever.

Gramma would not have approved.

But neither would she have approved the malign-
ing of my reputation, when it had been so long since
I'd had real, grown-up sex that my skin was begin-

ning to break out. I may not have been pure of spirit, but I was disgustingly underused of body.

I huffed my way west. Five minutes had me on my home block. I passed a gathering of fellow tenants on Fran's stoop two doors down from mine. Needless to say, I was not in the mood to schmooze and was up a stair toward my lobby door when I heard the attack.

"GOT ANOTHER ONE, HUH, BOWERING?"

Loony Lucy, one. Bowering, zero.

I turned on my heel in slo-mo, and did a beeline for the Old Yeller-murdering, Environmental Protection Act-violating Lucy. My last few hours of grilling were probably a direct result of her flapping mouth.

"HILLERMAN AND DAILY WEREN'T ENOUGH, WERE THEY? YOU HAD TO KILL WOOD, TOO, DIDN'T YOU?"

Okay, I was tense. It had not been my favorite day out of a month that was not my favorite out of a year that had, objectively sucked the big weenie.

I strode silently until I stood toe to toe with my accuser. There was spittle at the sides of Lucy's mouth, I noticed. It was not in the slightest bit difficult to imagine the demented woman in front of me slipping a pesticide shake to the passive—albeit equally demented—Mr. Hillerman. A vision of weeping red jelly flicked through my mind.

And I slapped Lucy with every ounce of strength I had, which even in my debilitated state was considerable. Fran gasped aloud. Several others applauded. Michelle sprang to action as the police car pulled up in front of the building; she put her arm around my waist and walked me toward my tenement. The cuts on my hand opened and started to bleed again.

I hoped Lucy wasn't rabid.

"What's going on here?" one of the patrolmen asked authoritatively.

"Our resident crazy is just at it again," Michelle answered with a winning smile, nodding over her shoulder to Lucy.

"SHE TRIED TO KILL ME," Lucy ranted. "RIGHT HERE IN FRONT OF EVERYBODY. ASK THEM. ASK THEM."

"What happened?" the cop asked the group.

"Nothing," Fran answered blandly. "Just Lucy going off again. Worse than a car alarm in the middle of the night."

"SHE KILLED THE OTHERS, TOO. SHE'S A MASS MURDERER AND SHE GYPPED ME OUT OF MY APARTMENT!"

Lucy had, in her enthusiasm, overstated her case.

Michelle walked me into the building as the eager witnesses all denied having seen anything at all, though they certainly wished they could be of help.

"That was very flashy," Michelle complimented me, once we were inside my apartment.

"Don't encourage me," I thanked her. "It'll only make me want to go pro."

She swabbed my hand with peroxide, and admired my fist. "Gee, I wish I'd done that," Michelle sighed, deadpan.

"Gee," I agreed, "I wish you had, too."

In the future, I'd have to remember to be sure it *was* someone else. At that moment, I had a bit more of the present to worry about than I'd intended.

And I was hungry.

For some reason, I wanted a doughnut.

TWELVE

That Evening

DURING A protracted period of apartment pacing, it occurred to me that my hangover had miraculously been healed. Praise be, my mind cleared and I had the energy to consider everything that had happened over the past three and a half days. As Mr. Feldstein had pointed out, nothing's worth crying about.

So, I examined the positive aspects of my situation. I had a good job offer. And? And I made myself a huge glass of chocolate milk and thought some more. So, I had a great job offer, and...Harvey Wood was dead. It was a shallow counting of my blessings, but I was making do.

The trouble with counting blessings is that it inevitably calls to mind the counting of curses—not that I'm superstitious, you understand. Naturally, I don't whistle backstage, or say the name of that "Scottish Play" by Shakespeare. I would never say "good luck" to a performer, or throw out my opening-night flowers before the show had closed. Nor would I dream of the curtain going up without giving a diva salute to my fellow cast members. And it would be unthinkable to fail to give everyone opening-night presents or ever allow the stage to go dark. Not to mention . . . oh, God.

Wood might be dead, but the Housing Court never sleeps. Landlords come and go, but eviction notices are forever. Nothing had changed for Jewel. In fact, with Wood dead, there was no person with enough authority to grant me a legal sublet so I could go off and take the country by storm. So, in fact, Jewel and I were in worse shape than before.

And who had killed Wood? I was pretty sure it wasn't me, but even I had to admit that evidence was piling up to the contrary. Not to mention a singular number of peripheral deaths in a six-building radius, great numbers of burglaries, and Loony Lucy spiking tuna juice in her hall.

Barry was taking my questioning seriously enough for both of us. Trying to tie me into every suspicious death over the past month would be stretching things too much for even a paranoid broad like me to consider at length. Of course, I have a rather short attention span. My credibility was in such a shambles, I wasn't about to start babbling to anyone about what was only a hunch about Lucy moving up to larger game. Shakespeare said quite a lot about protesting too much. So did Gramma.

On a petty note, my garden was history, and most of the people closest to me wanted me to discover some of the many wonders inside Bellevue—for my own good.

On the up side, I wasn't pregnant.

Of course, how could I be?

For a woman with the reputation of a slattern, I wasn't getting any action at all. If men weren't flatly rejecting my advances, they weren't making any either.

BLUBLUBLUB. The phone rang.

"Yes?"

"Vic, it's Brad."

Speaking of which—

"Yes."

"Busy?"

—unless they're married.

"No." I never learn. "What's cooking?"

"Well, Vic, the police blotter today mentioned something about your landlord, Harvey Wood, getting himself whacked in your basement this morning. Anything you can tell me about the investigation?"

"Maybe." An idea was forming. "Do you have any 'ins' at the ASPCA?"

A pause. "Maybe. Why?"

"There's been a complaint lodged against a woman named Lucy or Lucille in the building next door to mine. She's been poisoning dogs. Find out what kind of poison she's been using."

"Okay. Your turn."

"Brad, darling, I think I've finally figured out that I ought to wait for you to put up before I put out. Call when you have the name of that poison."

"Sweetheart—"

"Later, Brad."

"I think we should talk."

"We will, Brad. Later."

I hung up.

BLUBLUBLUB.

I picked up the phone and said, "Not until you come up with the goods, Brad. No more putting out. No more Ms. Nice Guy."

"Victoria Bowering?" the strange voice asked.

"Maybe. Who is this?"

"Oh, hi, Vic. This is Mike. I'm your stage manager for *Auntie Mame*. We still haven't got your contracts. Did you mail them? Because it's getting close to the wire here, and if you haven't, you'd better drop them in person at our office. In three days everything has to be at our lawyers' offices. You *did* get them, didn't you?"

"Oh, yes, I did, Mike." Now what? Tell him that as soon as I'm no longer under suspicion of murder I'll get back to him? That would certainly convince him of how much fun I'd be to have around for a year or so in strange cities here and in European countries without extradition treaties.

"If there's a problem, let me know; I'll do what I can. The producers already told your understudy, Fran, to start learning your lines. We really want to use you, Vic, but if it's about money, I'm afraid that's all she wrote."

"NO. No," I amended, "no problem. Just busy. You know. Busy, busy, busy."

He was thinking, oh shit, we hired Mary Tyler Moore. I know he was. Too late.

"So we can expect the signed contracts ASAP, yes?" Mike asked in that please-God-don't-let-her-be-another-diva-bitch voice.

"Of course!"

"Terrif!"

"Looking forward to it!"

"Me, too. Talk at 'cha later."

"*Ciao*."

"*Ciao*."

I closed up the frog belly, feeling for all the world like I was trapped in a very bad production of a Jean-Paul Sartre play.

Swallowing my pride with a very small gulp, I dialed Dan at home. No answer. I called his office. The guy at the next desk told me Duchinski had left early. I wasn't about to call his beeper number and allow him the privilege of not returning my call. Too pedestrian and humiliating, even for me. I take my humiliation man-to-man.

DUCHINSKI WAS RIGHT where I expected to find him (if not with me) at 8:30 on a Friday night: hunched over a Pimm's Cup at Miss Elle's Homesick Bar and Grill on Seventy-ninth Street. Two hundred and fifty pounds of glowering cop sat at the antique burnished bar sucking down a drink with enough fruit in it to keep a small third-world nation regular for a week. An intricate lace valance fluttered over the fan that tried to keep air circulating in the small bar area. The restaurant seemed busy, but I must have hit a cocktail lull.

I pulled up a rattan-backed stool and slid in next to Dan.

"Come here often?"

Dan didn't look up from the fascinating floating orange slices. "Not 'til now, you sweet-talking son-of-a-gun," he answered mechanically. "So," he finished his drink, pushed the empty forward for the bartender, and signaled another round and one for me, "how'd it go?"

"Soda, please," I ordered. The glum cloud enveloping Duchinski was dense. "I should probably be asking you. How *did* it go?"

"Not good, babe. Not so fuckin' good. And the answer to your next question is four." He took his fresh drink and held it in the air. "This one makes five."

Never had I seen Dan drink more than two. It frightened me more than any festive field trip to the Twentieth Precinct could.

"Dan?"

"No."

"You haven't heard my question," I protested.

"Wouldn't matter. If it's about us, no. If it's about the investigation, no. Can I help, whichever the arena, no. Even if the case were in my jurisdiction—which it isn't—it would be a blatant conflict of interest for me to interfere. For all the reasons I get called whenever you're in the soup, I'd get caught covering for you. No can do." He pushed his stool back. "Excuse me for a moment."

I watched him walk steadily back to the men's room. He hadn't looked at me once. Not in a mood to beat a dead horse, I picked up my coat and left the restaurant quietly. Like a good girl.

Maybe it was time to pack my bags and let the chips fall where they may.

The streets were calmer than usual, probably owing to the upcoming Halloween holiday which, in New York, is bigger than Christmas. People were resting up.

My suitcases were in the uppermost section of the bedroom closet at an elevation of ten to twelve feet. I moved Slasher off the scratching post he likes to nap on and balanced balletically atop it. By stretching two inches farther than biologically feasible, I reached the larger of the suitcases with the tips of my fingers and wiggled the corner of the baggage left to right and forward, millimeter by millimeter. I know this isn't practical storage, but it's more practical than finding room in a small apartment to keep a ladder. My job was further complicated by the fact that my luggage was the only place I had to store my off-season clothes, so each piece weighed about eighty thousand pounds.

What the hell. It wasn't like I had a *date* or anything. I worked the canvas back and forth and forward, and back and forth and forward.

BLUBLUBLUB.

The bag was coming forth.

BLUBLUBLUB.

The answering machine picked up the phone, and I had another inch of black upholstery fabric peeking out of the hidey-hole.

"BEEP. Hi, Vic. This is Dave Wood calling. I, uh, guess I should have known you'd have something to do on a Friday night, huh—?"

Yeah. Like killing myself on a carpeted piece of cat furniture. I grunted and got a finger hold on the elusive luggage.

"Anyway," Dave Wood's disembodied voice continued, "I was just thinking, uh, maybe we could get together and have some, uh, dinner this week. Or, uh, or, hey, a movie maybe—"

Ah-ha! I *had* it. Finally, in my hot little hand! Careful not to break a nail, I grasped both sides of the spiffy twenty-nine-inch Pullman with hidden roller wheels for easy lugging through Penn Station and heaved.

I am much stronger than I look.

Unfortunately, Slasher's scratching post is not. One side of the cylinder crumbled like a june bug on the windshield of a fast-moving Buick. Much the same way I hit the bedroom floor, except I caught the eight-thousand-pound Pullman, bull's eye on my upper chest. I would have said that it knocked the wind out of me, except I didn't have the wind to say it.

"Shit!" I did have the lung capacity for it, however.

Dave Wood's forgotten message ended with, "—so, get back to me at the office, or I'll just keep calling until I get you in person. Bye."

Slasher ambled over to where I lay on the floor, inspected his shattered playhouse, and licked my nose. Twice. Hard enough to abrade the skin.

Arghhhh. I chucked the case off my body and wove my way to the bathroom to inspect the damage in decent light. There were abrasions on both collarbones, scraped skin on the left. My redheaded complexion was going to show some beauts of bruises the next day and take two weeks to heal. Terrific.

BLAHHHHHHHHHHHHHHHHHHHHHHT.

Under no conditions was I going to be answering any doors that night. Or the phone. I was running away from home to join the circus and that was THAT.

BLAHHHHHHHHHHT. BLAHHHHHHHHHHHHHHHT.

I cleaned out the off-season clothes and started throwing the things I knew for sure I was going to need for a year on the road into the suitcase. One pile in the corner of the bedroom was for Goodwill Industries, another was for street people, another to be refolded for storage.

BLUBLUBLUB.

I took a Valium and packed.

BLAHHHHHHHHHHHHHHHHHHT.

I kept packing until the tranquilizer caught up with me. That was when I stopped throwing Slasher out of the suitcase and let him get to sleep.

The phone kept up long after the door buzzer quit. I plugged my ears and shut out the world. I was asleep five minutes after wriggling under the blankets.

I WAS BACK, reliving an old nightmare. It had been so long since I'd really slept, I resented it even in the fog of semiconsciousness. Dan was once again sitting on the edge of my bed, but this time he had my face in his hands and was rocking it back and forth. I struck at him to stop, but he grabbed my injured hand and it hurt.

Really hurt.

Consciously caused me pain.

Dan pulled out the earplugs.

"Jeez, Dan, we have to stop meeting like this."

"We have, Vic. Now listen to me, Vic, I am placing you under arrest for the murder of Harvey Wood. You have the right to remain silent. You have the right to have an attorney present during questioning. If you cannot afford an attorney, one will— "

At least Duchinski was looking at me again.

But what a look.

THIRTEEN

Saturday Morning, October 27

HOWEVER MUCH I thought I needed a change of scene, the holding cell at the conveniently located Twentieth Precinct was not quite the product of my late-night fantasies—even though I was assuredly receiving star treatment.

Sergeant Dan Duchinski, himself, personally checked me in to my spacious eight-by-eight cement-block suite. And not only did he make the phone call to Barry with his own quarter, he gallantly delivered a paper cup of the finest machine-made instant coffee available in the well-appointed, full-service station house.

The maître d'hotel—or desk sergeant, as she preferred to be called—pointed out the various amenities, including a toilet area *with* unlockable door (no chance of bothersome accidental police entrapment here) and *two,* not one, absolutely free telephone calls to the persons of my choice. Breakfast was presented promptly at seven A.M.: Croissan'wich (sausage and cheese, precisely as ordered), deep-fried shredded-potato brick, and extra-large piping-hot fresh-brewed Colombian coffee.

Recreation directors Franklin and Sawicki whisked me away as soon as I was settled for a relaxing review of my past indiscretions, as well as myriad options for my future entertainment. I just love games. Barry and I used to be very good at them, so it was my good fortune that he was along to play on my team.

Franklin went first.

"Do you know a Lucille Simmons?"

My turn.

"I know Lucille Ball." Barry kicked me under the fauxwood folding table. "I don't think so," I amended. Barry let out his breath.

"Residing at six-forty-five West Eightieth Street, apartment J?" Franklin continued for my edification.

"Loony Lucy? If it's Loony Lucy, yes, I know her. And no matter what she said, I have *not* had liposuction."

Barry kicked me again and asked Franklin where he was going with his line of questioning. I recrossed my legs.

"For broke," Franklin smiled. "Your apartment is being searched, so you may as well tell me; do you or have you had possession of the keys for the buildings and apartments owned by the deceased Harvey Wood?"

"I have my keys, yes. I don't have everybody else's keys, no." In the spirit of good fellowship, I paused for a bit. "Well, I have a spare set of keys for a few friends—Fran, Michelle, Jewel, you know—in case they misplace theirs or go out of town." Barry looked tense. He must have been searching for the leg I'd moved out of striking distance.

"So you have access to several of the buildings, besides yours. Okay. Like which ones?" Franklin prodded.

"Jeez, I don't know. As I said, Fran, Michelle, Jewel."

"That's quite a few."

"I'm president of the tenants' association." Barry found my hidden gams and gave me another love kick. "I happen to be very trustworthy, no matter what you hear from my more loosely wrapped neighbors."

"*You* tell *me* about Ms. Simmons."

I had the brains to look to Barry for permission, trusting him to find a way to covertly physically abuse me if I misspoke. He nodded, and I launched into the *Reader's Digest* version of my relationship with Sigmund Freud's failed lab project.

Yes, we had a "rocky" acquaintance. Yes, she accused me of embezzling funds from the tenants' association. Absolutely, I considered her crazier than a shithouse rat; they could ask anyone.

They had.

Okay. Perhaps, yes, it was *possible* that I had smacked Lucy—in public—hard enough to, just maybe, further rattle what passed for her brain.

Barry didn't kick me under the table. His hand grasped and squeezed my trick knee until I thought the joint would pop out of the socket. His face, however, remained perfectly composed as he asked Franklin exactly where he was leading.

"Oh, didn't I say?" Franklin asked innocently. "The super entered Ms. Simmons apartment about an hour ago to investigate an overrunning bathtub and discovered your client's recent sparring partner lying on the living room floor, dead as a cheap battery."

Now, until that moment, I had always considered fainting to be somewhat melodramatic. "Less is more" remains my acting credo. Nonetheless, the blood dropped from my head like an elevator car with a snapped cable.

In my own defense, one of the most annoying things about the human mind is its ability to process volumes of disparate information in less time than blood pressure takes to cope. I was *not* being a wimp.

Anyway, the light-headedness passed in a few seconds, and I can proudly say that I was not inelegant enough to fall over.

Barry asked, "What was the cause of death?"

"Asphyxiation," Franklin answered. "Of course, that's preliminary, but the victim had bruising around the mouth and her skin was bluer than Frank Sinatra's eyes." I must have stuck a cigarette in my mouth without thinking, because Sawicki lit it.

"And, I couldn't help noticing, Ms. Bowering that you have some bruises yourself."

Involuntarily, I looked down to the neckline of the oversized cotton top I'd thrown on. It had slipped over one shoulder exposing an expanse of black-and-blue marks. They did not look good, cosmetically or legally.

"We will be questioning you later about the deaths of a Mr. Tom Daily and Mr. Sam Hillerman—also acquaintances of yours. Also both possibly whacked. Digitalis was found in high concentrations in Hillerman's blood." Franklin stood and finished, "And he didn't have a prescription. That's all for now. There is a policewoman and photographer waiting outside for Ms. Bowering. Mr. Laskin," Franklin added, "you know, if it weren't for Ms. Simmons's getting iced, I'd think your wife here had a real specific mad-on for men."

I'VE ALWAYS HATED photo shoots, and I'd never even had one done without my shirt. I wouldn't be asking for reprints for my portfolio.

The assault and battery I'd taken at the hands of my matched luggage had turned my upper arms and chest into a Calder painting of broken blood vessels and lumps. I looked as if I'd just gotten home from dinner with Mike Tyson—or, more pertinently, had recently subdued a recalcitrant strangulation victim.

I did not say "cheese," though it did occur to me.

Barry gallantly accompanied me to my arraignment downtown in the toenail of Manhattan. The judge was extremely agreeable. She agreed that there certainly *was* a reason to hold me over for trial. She even agreed with Barry that it was apparent to anyone with the IQ of a bowl of Rice Krispies that I had neither resources nor any place to go, so bail was set at a measly five thousand dollars. A bargain.

Dan was waiting in my luxurious holding tank, anyway.

Try getting that kind of service at the Ritz Carlton.

"Anybody ever tell you that you have shitty karma?" Dan asked, offering me a lit cigarette and making room for my weary butt on the cozy cot thoughtfully suspended from the wall. That's when I shut down.

When I didn't speak or move toward him, Dan went on, "The judge gave you a break on bail, but you're probably going to have to spend the night anyway. I brought you a Larry McMurtry novel, junk food, extra cigarettes, the name of a good bail bondsman—but don't use one at all, if you can avoid it. If there's anything I forgot, Fran said she'd be happy to bring it. She feels pretty bad about queering your alibi with that phone message. We'll work it out, Vic."

I couldn't get a thank-you past my lips, only stared dumbly at the cop within my cell and the passing cops without. "Barry's taking care of it."

Gramma would have been so embarrassed at my lapse of manners.

Seeing me without a coffin nail in my mouth must have worried Dan. He heaved himself off the cot and brought the butt over to me by the barred wall, and stuck it between the fingers of my right hand. It slipped from my grasp, and I bent to retrieve it, but Dan crushed it quickly under his shoe.

"Don't smoke that, baby. God only knows what's been on that floor."

I couldn't avert my blank gaze from the broken body of the one-hundred-twenty-millimeter menthol, smoldering on the concrete. Not that it was that fascinating, I just couldn't think of anything else to do with my eyes. They didn't seem to have the energy to weep productively as directed.

"Vic? Vic? I'm going to have to go pretty soon. Is there anything else you need?"

Was there anything else I needed? Let's see. There was the full-length mink coat I had to sell to pay the rent. There was the month in Vienna I would have found mildly distracting. Dinner and dancing with Sean Connery might have been nice. On the other hand, an alibi would have been festive, too.

Duchinski folded me in his arms and held tight, rocking rhythmically in tiny, slow nods, my head and hands tucked compactly beneath his unshaven chin. As my frayed muscles relaxed, Dan firmly rubbed the length of my spine with his left hand until the tears arrived.

The corollary between my position and that of a colicky baby being burped was not wasted on me, which meant my synapses were once again firing.

Dan gallantly mopped up my face and sat me down.

"I have to go now, Vic. Slasher could use some reassurance while the white shields toss your apartment. Then Barry and I are getting together to map out a defense strategy. You shouldn't be in here for more than a night, so try to relax."

I didn't mean to laugh, but I did.

"Yeah, well, it *is* quieter here than in my apartment." I ran my fingers down Dan's stubbly cheek. "I thought you couldn't do anything for me."

"I couldn't. I decided to take some of my vacation time. A couple of days. What the hell. I've been a little tense lately. Didn't want to burn out."

"Nah. Wouldn't want that." I did want to kiss him very badly: a long, slow one, with face rubbing and neck nuzzling. And then a protracted nap.

Dan called to be let out, released me, and said, "Oh. I got this out of your personal property bag up front." He pulled a yellow five-by-ten booklet from his back pocket. "It's your *Auntie Mame* script. Might as well make good use of your time, huh?"

A black female police officer released the lock on the cage. I wanted to tell Dan that I loved him, but I somehow knew that was the last thing he needed to hear in a jail cell, so I waved him off cavalierly.

And wondered if, gratitude aside, it might have been true. Or if it was just a variation on the old "Stockholm syndrome."

EXCEPT FOR MY being summarily incarcerated in the slammer, the remainder of the evening passed rather mundanely. My thoughts were twirling like gerbils in Habitrails. Nothing new there, except there were a *lot* of gerbils, and they were more important gerbils than usual. As would be expected, none of them ever got anywhere except back to the beginning of the maze.

Barry dropped by with a one-pound bag of dark chocolate pecan turtles from the Broadway Nut Shop, and the news that my bail had been knocked down to four thousand dollars with the condition that I be released into Duchinski's personal custody. I signed the power of attorney papers that would authorize Barry to clean out my paltry IRA account to cover the 10 percent required.

After a dinner of chicken-fried steak, mashed potatoes, and okra (which I defiantly left on my plate), Omar Salim's personage appeared through my bars to offer condolences and an armful of Rubrum lilies. I was beginning to feel like a misunderstood political terrorist with social connections.

Since a four-hundred dollar IRA wouldn't hold me for more than forty-five minutes of old age anyway, I passed on Omar's offer of making bail.

"You have pride," Omar commented. "I find that charming."

"Thank you."

"Your friend Susie also tells me you are a gifted psychic fortune-teller." I didn't point out that a "gifted" psychic might not find herself cooling her heels in the big house. An M.I.T. grad such as Omar would surely grasp the irony. "Perhaps I could persuade you to predict the future of a few friends I am entertaining tomorrow evening. For your usual fee, of course. I would be most grateful."

Hmmmm.

"Contingent upon my release or escape, naturally."

"Naturally."

Hmmmm.

Palmistry and tarot readings make me very nervous, partially because I'm not a charlatan and it's very hard work. Partially because I have to open up a lot to give a valid projection, and my neurotic self-examination gets out of control. Partially because that niggling ethical part of me doesn't believe in charging money for information that is, at best, 80 percent reliable.

I weighed poverty against another puny drop of tension in a tidal wave of anxiety.

"One hundred fifty dollars for the first hour, one hundred for every hour after, three-hour maximum. After that I'm useless."

"That, I very much doubt." Omar reached for my hand through the food tray opening in the bars, and brought it to his lips. "We will be charmed. The

dinner will be in the private dining room at the Château d'Or at eight-thirty tomorrow evening. I will
send a car for you.''

"Time's up," Policewoman Garcia said, tapping
Omar's shoulder. He kissed my hand one more time
and made his exit. "You have some weird life,"
Garcia commented. "If you beat this thing, we
should have lunch some time."

I memorized lines until lights out.

Well, I tried.

FOURTEEN

Sunday Morning, October 28

MY EARLY-MORNING RELEASE from the neighborhood penal institution of choice bore all the characteristics of a small-town parade. Barry arrived to sign sundry papers and deliver money; Dan presented himself shortly after with Fran and Michelle in tow. Though Omar Salim did not appear himself, his limo and driver did, with instructions to wait however long it took for me to be formally sprung. I thought it was a sweet sentiment which was totally wasted on Dan and Barry. Nonetheless, we all piled into the rear of the stretch for the four-minute trip to my apartment.

"Why do they always darken the glass in limos?" Fran asked. I could see visions of her portrayal of Auntie Mame dancing in her head. I decided it would be over my dead body. Then I decided that was a poor choice of phrasing, given the circumstances.

"Privacy," Dan grunted, giving Fran a look as if she'd flunked nursery school. Twice.

Michelle rolled down her window at the same moment Fran did. Sandwiched between the two glowering men in the cheap seats riding backward, I leaned over Barry—the thinner of the two—and hit the toggle to open the sunroof.

"What's the point of being driven around in a limo if no one knows it?" Fran asked. In unison, Fran and Michelle stuck their heads out the two windows while I stood to push my face through the sunroof. Dan pulled me back to my seat. I bounced back up long enough to wave at McAleer's, on the off-chance that someone would recognize me. It was very satisfying and briefly took my mind off the various parts of my body that were throbbing. Barry glowered. Dan heaved a sigh and looked skyward in exasperation.

"Female bonding," Barry explained unnecessarily. Dan ignored him.

All of us were classy enough to wait for the chauffeur to open the doors for us to spill out at my door, however.

Barry stood by the limousine and said, "If you don't mind, I have to get to the office." Dan nodded approval as though I weren't there, and Barry crawled back into the car and rode off. With the remainder of my entourage I went inside. Michelle made coffee, Fran called her service, Dan and Slasher did some male bonding, and I took a bath. By the time I was dry, dressed, and back in the living room, the group was tearing into a Zabar's bag of lox, cream cheese, bagels, Brie, and French bread. The coffee was already gone, so I made another pot as Dan ripped a garlic bagel with a *schmeer* into bite-sized pieces for the cat.

"So, Michelle, you have custody," Dan instructed.

"Of what?" I asked.

"Of whom," Michelle corrected, picking bread crumbs from the lap of her Chanel suit. "You."

Before I could assert my ability to take care of myself—head stuck through sunroof notwithstanding—Dan preempted me: "Yes, you do." Then turning to Michelle, he asked, "You can take a few days off work if you have to?"

"The world of advertising can live without me," she nodded, spreading cheese on a slice of baguette.

"Wait a minute," I protested. "I don't want anyone losing work over this mess. Even if I needed a bodyguard—which I don't—why not Fran? She doesn't have a day job to jeopardize."

"Fran is a flake," Dan said without malice. Fran smiled through a mouthful of bagel in affirmation.

"What about Susie, then?" I asked.

Fran, Michelle, and Dan just shook their heads in benign amazement.

"Fran," Dan went on, "your job is to schmooze the neighborhood and find out whatever you can. Take notes. Maybe you can find out who's been making those calls."

"What calls?" I asked.

"Oh, I guess I forgot to tell you while you were in the lockup," Fran said as she rifled through my roll-top desk looking for a pad of paper and a pen. "I got a threatening phone call Friday night telling me that I'm 'next.' Just like the ones that Harvey Wood reported you making. That's why I called so many times." She located the paper and closed the desk. "Since I couldn't be sure that it was a man's voice, the police think it was you. Sorry."

"What? How could they?"

Michelle looked sympathetic. "I told you to quit smoking, Vic. You're beginning to sound like a cross between Lauren Bacall and Divine, that transvestite actor. Anyway, according to the blotter, you have a track record."

"Thank you, Ms. Clean." I lit a cigarette, noticing how much I sounded like Divine. "Divine's dead."

"Precisely," Michelle maturely confirmed.

Thank you, Nanny-dearest.

"Speaking as the fuzz," Dan interjected, "our big problem here is that once cops decide they have the bad guy, we stop looking around for anybody else to nail for the dirty deed. And there's enough circumstantial evidence slamming Vic to satisfy any jury I've ever seen."

"Oh, God," I mumbled, jumping to my feet.

"Don't worry, Vic," Fran reassured me. "I'll send postcards from the road."

"Exactly!" I said over my shoulder and on my way to the dreaded answering machine. I punched the Play button.

"BEEP. Bowering, this is Mike your stage manager. The producers are having cows, bulls and buffaloes. Where the fuck is your contract?"

"BEEP. Welcome home, beautiful one. This is Omar. I hope my car was convenient for you. I also wanted to confirm how very much I and my guests are looking forward to seeing you this evening. Of course, if you are too tired—" I turned the machine off. Too late, naturally.

"No," Dan enunciated clearly from the living room.

"I need the money, Dan," I argued, digging through the mess in my desk.

"Vic!" Fran exclaimed in horror.

"That's not what she means," Dan explained even though I hadn't told him what *I* meant.

"It's a fortune-telling gig," I muttered. "Where the hell did I put that contract?"

"No, anyway," Dan insisted. "No to the psychic shit—I guess we both know where that trip leads—and an emphatic no to the contract. The white shields who came through your apartment were thrilled enough to see your bags packed for an extended trip on the lam. No."

"They'd know where to find me," I argued.

"No contract. No, dammit."

"Is this a conspiracy to bankrupt me?"

Dan gripped my arm too hard. "This is a conspiracy to keep you off death row."

Such a convincing complication slowed me down some. Adrenaline is a dangerous thing in the hands of a professional actor.

"Personally," Fran said, lowering a slice of lox into her mouth, "I think a man did it. Women don't strangle people, do they?"

"That's right!" Michelle offered with enthusiasm.

Dan was not impressed. "Nor do women generally punch other women out, do they Vic? Most especially not on busy Manhattan streets in the presence of a dozen witnesses one knows personally."

Ouch. Got me.

"Wait a minute," Michelle demanded, "there are several men we ought to consider here. For one, what about Wood's son, David? He had lots to gain from bumping off the old man: all the rental properties, insurance, the estate—"

"Me," I grimaced.

"Don't tell me," Dan begged.

"I didn't do anything!" I defended myself. "Somehow David Wood got the idea that his father and I were having an affair. He called and left a message asking me out."

"But isn't that good?" Michelle asked, leaning forward and looking every inch the advertising creative type. "First of all, David inherited. Terrific. And if David Wood believed that his father was keeping Vic, a possession he obviously coveted, wouldn't that be yet another motive for him to fry daddy?"

Dan looked interested. "Vic, do you still have that message?"

Sheepishly, I answered, "No. I erase the messages every time. It's a habit."

"Damn," he said. "Break the habit. Anything you get from now on I want to hear." He caught himself and looked askance in my direction. "Excuse me. Don't *want* to hear, but need to." Slasher let out a loud catch of a snore as if in support of his buddy the cop.

"If you ask me," Fran offered, "I think there's something fishy about Ahab the Arab and Ivan, too. Mohammed there wants to buy these buildings, though I can't imagine why—"

"I can," Dan said accusingly at me.

"—and," Fran continued, "there's something just plain spooky about Ivan. I mean, why would a kind of attractive, apparently educated man of his age be interested in subletting a pissant, dark hole like this at all?"

Since Fran had a point, I didn't even bother to look offended.

Fran was on a roll and went on, "But you know who *I* think killed both Wood and Lucy?" Timing being everything, she did not pause for a response. "Jewel LaFleur."

I almost choked on a lungful of smoke. Michelle laughed aloud. Dan must have lost his appreciation of the ludicrous because he urged Fran further. "How so?"

"Well," Fran warmed to the subject, "a lot of things. Jewel has spent the last ten years locked in that apartment of hers. The place gets even less sun than yours, Vic. Two days, let alone a decade, on sensory deprivation would be enough to make most people flip out. Wood was working like a demented elf trying to get her thrown out onto the street; why wouldn't that make her crazy?"

"Because it *wouldn't*," I defended.

"Everyone knows Jewel has master keys for all the buildings," Michelle contributed apologetically. "And if Mr. Hillerman and Daily were murdered, too, wouldn't it have to have been done by someone who is psychotic, instead of just unstable like Vic?"

My heart pounded in my chest. If there's one thing my metabolism reacts poorly to, it's bald-faced logic. But then I remembered the obvious. Matching pragmatic argument for pragmatic argument, I said, "Nobody was killed in Jewel's apartment. And, as you said, she has been *housebound* for as long as any of us has known her. Besides, what possible motive could she have?"

Dan had the courtesy to appear sorry for me before saying, "Just because she hasn't left her house in ten years or more doesn't mean she doesn't know everything that's going on in the neighborhood." I felt as though I'd been slapped. Dan continued. "You tell Jewel everything, Vic. She loves you like a lioness loves her cub. Forget Jewel's problems with Wood; do you think for a second that there is a thing in the world that she wouldn't do to protect you? She was on the phone when Lucy accused you of embezzlement at the tenants' meeting. Maybe she thought you were going buggers because of the pressure of waiting on Mr. Hillerman.''

''Me?''

''A week ago, you had three burrs in your side: Hillerman, Wood, and Loony Lucy. Two major burrs, Vic. One minor. Now you have none. Who might be protective enough to get rid of them?''

I shook my head, trying to come up with another defense and feeling guilty for beginning to see the logic. But then, I've never been one to let rational thinking get in my way. ''What about the man making the threatening phone calls?''

Fran rather smugly asserted, ''I said I wasn't *sure* it was a man. Jewel was a performer. Any one of the three of us could lower our voices enough to camouflage our sex, and Michelle's been out of the business for years and doesn't even smoke. Jewel even lives in Lucy and Daily's building. She might have had her own reasons for offing Daily. No matter how out of shape the murderer, a couple of floors isn't much. Let's face it, Jewel outweighed Lucy by several hundred pounds. Tom Daily, too. If it isn't you, Vic, it has to be Jewel.''

I was speechless. The only sound in the apartment was Slasher's rhythmic snoring. Where was Julio when I finally needed him?

"Sorry, babe," Dan murmured. Then reverting to the cop he was, he took the professional track again. "This is good stuff. Fran, you'd better go do what you have to. Find out whatever gossip you can about the stiffs, and keep what you know to yourself. You haven't exactly been circumspect, so far. I'm going to go call in a few favors from my friends and enemies alike. Michelle, don't you turn your back on the redhead. She may be innocent, but she's devious as hell."

Some support group I had there.

"Do we have to stay in all the time?" Michelle asked for no obvious reason.

"Not as long as you don't let Vic out of your sight," Dan answered.

"Good," Michelle smiled in my direction. "Then Vic can do the fortune-telling job tonight."

Dan's shoulder slumped. I could almost hear his silent count from one to ten.

"Omar's sending a car," I added, "and the party's in a popular four-star restaurant."

Dan moved the sleeping cat from his lap to the coffee table and stood. "All right, all right. But don't leave Vic's side for an instant, you hear? Don't even go to the ladies' room alone—," he opened the door to leave, "—not that that should be a problem for you two. C'mon Fran, let's blow this pop stand."

Fran grabbed a bagel for the road and followed the vacationing cop into the hall.

I toasted Michelle with my coffee mug and shouted after Dan, "What? No good-bye kiss?" He didn't even turn around to reject me.

"Cops shouldn't be so quick to judge who's the devious one," Michelle congratulated herself on the way to another cup of coffee.

I reached for the phone. "I think I'll call Jewel," I said.

Michelle took the receiver from my hand and said, "I think not. Much as I'm far too young to be your mother, I think for today you'd better stop acting like a child. Get your outfit together for tonight. I've been wanting to get into the Château d'Or for as long as I've been in New York, and you're not going to screw it up for me. Then the two of us will go to my apartment while I choose my tasteful yet provocative ensemble. Agreed?"

"Agreed." I inadvertently remembered a promise I had made to myself about eight kazillion times to listen to Michelle, the smart one of the broad brigade—not to mention the spiffiest dresser.

When the phone rang, Michelle snatched up the receiver before I could get to it. After a second, she handed it over.

"It's Brad."

"Brad, what have you got?"

"A strong desire to take you to dinner."

"Funny. What was in the tuna?"

"Githagin and saponin glycosides."

"Is that anything like digitalis?"

"The heart stimulant?" Brad asked. "No. The poison that killed the dogs was a depressant. Probably organic, though they haven't established that for a certainty. Totally different poisons. So," I could almost hear Brad's pencil poised, "what have you got for me?"

"I was arraigned yesterday for Wood's murder."

"What? How did I miss that?"

"I guess you were too busy with the ASPCA. Thanks." I hung up, disgusted.

"What was that about?" Michelle asked.

"I was checking to see if the poison that killed Hillerman was the same as the one Lucy was using on the dogs. Not even close."

"Good try," Michelle complimented me. "But now Lucy's dead, too. I'd like to think she strangled herself to death, but I'm not that gullible. And I just don't see Wood as a poisoner—not even to empty an apartment where he could up the rent. Sorry."

I was, too. So far we had death by poison, electrocution, gunshot (maybe self-inflicted), and strangulation. Whoever our culprit was, he was versatile. I considered hauling out every review I'd ever gotten that had accused me of being a one-note actress. That ought to clear my name. But I was already too depressed to go *looking* for bad reviews. Just for the moment I wanted to forget all of it, and primp my brains out.

Besides, I had the strongest feeling that Château d'Or was going to be serving up a lot more than cordon bleu that night, and—as all my friends know— when I suppress those feelings, they only give me, and everyone around me, gas.

FIFTEEN

Sunday Evening, October 28

OMAR SALIM'S limousine was waiting right on time. Michelle and I pretended to have forgotten something in the apartment, giving the neighbors a better opportunity to appreciate our unbelievable coolness. We had to do it twice more until Mrs. O'Hara next door came out to dump her recyclables and complain about morons with more money than brains double-parking on *her* street. Gratified that we'd been properly noticed, we gave up and got into the Mercedes.

"Don't touch that window!" I stopped Michelle mid-roll down. "You have perma-pressed hair; I do not. It took me and my curling iron the last hour to arrange my head and I don't want to show at Château d'Or looking like an explosion in a mattress factory." Michelle shrugged good-naturedly so I, per my nature, felt guilty at robbing her of her chance at being a transitory shooting star through the streets of Manhattan, and conceded, "But we'll both open windows at red lights." Michelle grinned happily.

Actors may retire and go into advertising, but they never quite grow up.

"How's your French?" Michelle asked, pouring herself a glass of white wine from the stocked bar to her left. "The Château d'Or is so snotty even the busboys refuse to speak English." She inspected the label on the bottle before returning it to its place. "I like that. It reminds me that I had the balls to leave Massachusetts."

"Je comprends, mais je ne parle pas très bien," I responded as offhandedly as I could manage, *"La prononciation est un peu difficile pour moi."*

I didn't spend my summers working in restaurants and not getting tipped by the Quebecois back in New Hampshire for nothing.

"Bien sûr," Michelle shot back, not one to be outdone.

Rather than drive down the West Side and then eastward, the driver took us through Central Park at Seventy-ninth Street and down Second Avenue toward the United Nations area and Château d'Or—which is pretty much where all the outrageously priced French restaurants are located. I've always chalked that up to diplomats' having difficulty quickly calculating the exchange rate. Let's face it, an Italian used to paying in the tens of thousands of lira is not going to think twice about a side salad priced at fifteen lousy dollars.

Michelle had chosen to wear a white crepe suit with small rhinestone buttons, gray shoes, and tiny purse. I, in typical fashion desperation, wore what I always did on the rare occasions that someone might care:

a gold sueded silk scoop-neck sheath cut on the bias
with matching kimono jacket and high heels. I would
have worn lower heels to avoid any unintentional
emotional castration of short men, but Fayva didn't
have any in the right color. My purse, of course, was
as big as a beach cottage to accommodate my tarot
deck, crystal ball, and two packs of cigarettes. I
plucked Slasher's hairs off the fabric and rolled them
into discreet balls as we rode. It kept my hands busy
since, in deference to Michelle, I didn't smoke. And
I was wound tighter than a cheap watch.

The Château d'Or doorman opened the limousine door with a smooth, *"Bon soir, mademoiselle et
madame."* Rather than ask which one of us looked
older, I *bon-soir*ed him back. He led us to the maître
d' who promptly sized us up and asked if we were
"deux." I wanted to inform him that I am rarely
deux with another woman, but words failed me.
They always do when food service personnel give me
that, "you're a hooker, aren't you?" look and I'm
operating with foreign *mots.*

"Monsieur," Michelle asked, *"nous sommes ici
pour la partie de Monsieur Salim. C'est où, s'il vous
plâit?"* Well done, I thought. So did Monsieur, who
immediately led us over thick tapestry carpets to the
upstairs private dining rooms.

"Merci," I tossed off when we'd reached our des-
tination. Then to Michelle, I added, "He thinks
we're hookers."

"C'est vrai," Michelle agreed, looking over the plethora of tuxedoed men in the room, "but he thinks we're really *expensive* hookers." I tried to appreciate the distinction and succeeded. "Look at those guys," she gushed. "I haven't seen so many straight men in one New York room in, well, *ever.*"

"What makes you so sure they're straight?"

"Ivan is."

"What?" Sure enough, standing taller than all the rest of the assembly, looking for all the world like Hungarian royalty, was Ivan, the McAleer's bartender. His tuxedo was obviously custom-made—and recently, too. As Omar Salim made his way toward Michelle and me, Ivan caught sight of us and made a raised-eyebrow European nod of acknowledgment. A jolt of unpleasant coincidence crawled up from my stomach. Ivan Stepanek seemed inordinately amused at my surprise, so I crooked my eyebrow back at him. But I didn't mean it.

"You know," Michelle interrupted my crooking, "I haven't seen you so relaxed in months. Just because nothing was happening, you were losing your mind. Now that you've been dumped by your husband and boyfriend, been threatened with eviction, and arrested for serial murder, you've never looked better." She smiled at the approaching Omar and finished from behind her upturned lips, "Has anyone ever told you that you may be psychotic?"

"You mean besides you?"

"Uh-huh."

"Yes. I have a very open and honest family."

"I don't think it's healthy for you to block your emotions."

"Which ones?" I asked, finally having decided that Ivan and Omar could have gotten to know one another at the tenants' meeting. Both were gregarious, pleasant men.

"Fear of incarceration, eviction, electrocution. All those 'shun' words."

"I'm not blocking my emotions," I said while doing so.

"Bull*merde*," Michelle disagreed bilingually within a single word. "You're blocking."

Omar Salim joined us before Michelle could further impugn my dubious mental health, and kissed both of our right hands.

"How truly beautiful you both look this evening. I must apologize that the room cannot do either of you justice."

Or vice versa. The walls were papered in a loden green silk paper, accented by pale cream enamel on the heavily ornamented ceiling and moldings. Mid-nineteenth-century oil paintings hung beneath individual lights. The tablecloths were also a rich cream brocade; matching brocade napkins folded into the shape of swans floated ethereally in the center of heavily gold-rimmed china. The flicker of candles in baroque brass candlesticks reflected sedately off the polished crystal wine glasses. Three to a setting.

Great. My prognostications are always much more on the money when my audience is ripped to the tits.

"Will you do me the honor of sitting to my right, Victoria?" Omar asked. "And Madame, I have seated you to the right of Ambassador Renchenkov." He leaned confidentially closer to Michelle's ear, "The poor man has recently lost his wife, and the only companion who might divert him would be one as sophisticated and charming as you." At least I was relieved to know that it was Michelle who was called *madame* by the maître d'. "Sophisticated" is an accepted cosmopolitan euphemism for "older than the other one."

Michelle shot into actress mode—the one I *thought* she'd retired—smoothly, without a hitch. "Alexis Renchenkov, the retired Olympian athlete?" Omar nodded sympathetically. "Of course, Omar. I'd be happy to help."

"Please excuse me for one moment. My last guest has arrived," Omar said to Michelle, squeezing her hand in profound gratitude.

"We're getting *fed*," Michelle enthused in a whisper. "I feel like I've died and gone to the NFL."

"Really," I huffed a bit, "food and sex. I thought you got out of acting."

"Yeah, well. You can take the girl out of acting, but you can't always get the acting out of the girl. Let's mingle our brains out before you have to be the hired help." She grabbed my arm and turned me just enough to see Omar greet his late guest. It was David Wood.

This soiree was rapidly becoming the second weirdest party I'd ever attended. The only thing at the first to edge out this bizarre assembly was that other guest of honor ended up more lifeless than an Ali McGraw performance.

"You circulate," I ordered Michelle. "I'm going to check the place cards."

Ivan stopped me with a terribly chic air kiss to my cheek, and, "I'm to your right, Ms. Bowering. I hope you're as pleased as I am."

"More," I offered, stealing a glance at the direction that David Wood was taking into the room. There was much glad-handing all around. "I don't want to be crass," I said to Ivan, "but what the hell are you doing here?"

"Same as you. Business," he answered cryptically. Ivan handed me a glass of champagne, introduced me to myriad men with unpronounceable names, one woman in a Muslim thobe, and another who looked like a young vice-president of IBM.

My instincts were humming like a tuning fork.

"She's a hooker," Ivan informed me, "special for the Tunisian chargé d'affaires."

"Who's the other woman?" I asked.

"The wife of the Tunisian chargé d'affaires."

"I don't want to pry, Ivan, but how does a bartender at McAleer's know all these people on a first-name basis?"

"That *would* be prying, though, wouldn't it?" he deflected. "However, before my fall from grace, I traveled a much wider circle."

"You're stonewalling me, Ivan. That makes me curious. There's not a person in this room who would tend bar anywhere, let alone want to sublet my unchic little hovel. The hooker wouldn't even live there."

"She wouldn't have any reason to," Ivan said teasingly, and lit us both cigarettes, putting an end to that train of conversation. His composure was frightening in a way I couldn't quite pinpoint.

Through the events of the past several days I had not fully considered the incongruities of Ivan's or Omar's sudden appearance in my admittedly lower-middle-class niche of Upper West Side society. As obvious as the nose on Charles de Gaulle's face was the fact that both men had turned up on the same damned day. Ivan had been around longer than Omar, but only in McAleer's—not in my face. There was a Batman and Robin quality to the coincidence that struck a not-so comic note.

I left my face as implacable as Ivan's all the way through the seven-course dinner. When I'm listening hard, my face forgets to move—except to chew, naturally.

Omar and Ivan were the most charming of dinner companions, from escargots through Spanischew-indetorte. It was not lost on me that that sort of elan takes a bit of practice. Every so often I caught snippets of conversation coming from the second large round table, the most jarring of which was what sounded like a damned-well-put-together sentence from Michelle in Russian. When I looked up from my lemon sorbet, David Wood was staring intently in my direction. He was wearing his newfound wealth well. His face had taken on an aggressive jut since I last saw him in front of the Twentieth Precinct. Once, twice, three times a lady, I grinned with embarrassment and saluted him gracelessly.

I leaned casually toward Omar and asked, "I didn't realize that you knew David Wood."

"Excuse me?" Omar's brow furrowed, then smoothed. "Ah, yes, your new landlord. My dear Vic, in my business I must know many people."

Ivan's short laugh pierced the classical background music, which, in turn, pulled a chuckle from Omar. Something was going on, but I wasn't going to get any help at this table. Perhaps that was why I was seated where I was. Oops. Paranoia, again.

"Have you been to Beirut recently?" Omar asked.

Despite the arrival of dessert, my attention was snagged. Before I could come up with a snappy response to such an obvious setup, Ivan answered, which was very, very good. To ask if I wanted a little more information would be comparable to asking if I had any interest in taking home a doggie bag.

"Unfortunately not," Ivan said, exchanging his untouched slice of Viennese pastry for my empty plate. "I'm afraid banking hasn't been very good for me recently."

"A shame for all of us." Omar turned to me. "Ivan is not only a brilliant economist but, as you have surely noticed, an excellent conversationalist in several languages." He approved the maître d's choice of cognac. "Perhaps banking will be good for you again, soon."

"Perhaps," Ivan agreed, accepting a slim cigar from Omar—who to his credit offered me one as well. I chose to finish his dessert instead. "You might enjoy one, Victoria," Ivan urged, smiling. "They're Havana."

Why did that not surprise me? Which, in turn, reminded me of the reason I was sitting where I was.

"Omar, dinner was fabulous, but I think I should get started working, don't you?" Of course, I could have lived my entire life without looking at another tarot deck, but that New England sense of responsibility—the one that says that pleasure always has a cost—had been drummed into me pretty damned hard. It is my least favorite sense.

As Jewel LaFleur always told me: "Anything worth doing is worth getting paid for; and anything worth having is worth getting free."

"Of course," Omar said. "There is a table set up for you right there," he pointed to a charming corner with a small round table and two Louis Quatorze chairs. Three white tapers burned in the center of the table. Omar had obviously had his tarot done before. Michelle laughed musically and demurred *Spasibah* to Ambassador Renchenkov. I cursed the day I convinced Omar that I had pride, and grabbed my bag. Something stunk at the Château d'Or, and I guessed I'd do about anything to find out what was rotten.

"Omar, may I read you first? It will make the others more comfortable."

"Of course," he said, holding my chair.

As I squeezed past Michelle she caught the hem of my dress and asked, "How are your vibes?"

Leaning discreetly to her, I admitted, "Weird. I suddenly don't have any."

"I told you," Michelle pronounced unsympathetically, "you're blocking."

Maturely, I responded, "Am NOT. This is an uncommon situation, that's all. I was fine a minute ago, and I'll be fine a minute from now. All I have to do is concentrate."

Once Omar and I were seated opposite one another, I placed the crystal ball in its stand, removed the tarot cards from their silk scarf wrapping, and swept them over the top of the candle flames. These are rules; I don't know why, but they are—and I am, if nothing else, a creature of habit. I shuffled, and Omar cut the cards the requisite three times without being instructed. All the while I tried to pick up some of the Arab's "vibrations," or read his body language, or do whatever the hell it is that earns me the big bucks for telling people about themselves and being right most of the time.

Nothing.

I had Omar cut the cards again.

Nothing.

I felt as though my stomach would fall through my lower gastrointestinal tract. You see, the way I read the tarot, the cards are nothing more than props. I get impressions and interpret the pretty cardboard to coordinate with what I feel. This works really well for God-only-knows why, except for those occasions when my receptors are getting nothing but a station identification.

I smiled ingratiatingly. Omar smiled back encouragingly. Ambassador Renchenkov turned his chair around to eavesdrop. David Wood crossed his arms and stared.

So okay, all right, fine, I was blocked tighter than a carnivore on a Kaopectate diet. It wasn't like it was the first time it had happened to me. It's just that usually no one was paying such close attention. Except it *was* the first time, and my public was *riveted*. If nothing else, I could predict with 100 percent accuracy, a very long evening ahead. Naturally, I did the professional thing under the circumstances: I did my best to evaluate clothing, posture, and what I'd overhead; lied my brains out; and tried to make it funny.

My luck was that Omar was too much of a gentleman to disagree with anything I said; it was obvious that Renchenkov would laugh at anything *anyone* said; and this particular group wasn't especially interested in fortune-telling. My sixth sense is usually all over me like excema, and just when a little flaking and itching was needed—a MIRACLE—I was cured. I blamed Michelle for having brought the idea up in the first place, and slogged workmanlike through the short line of curiosity seekers.

Brazen was the watchword with Omar.

"You and Ivan are in New York in the same capacity, but different jobs," I stated confidently. He didn't budge an inch, so I continued. "Your professions couldn't seem more different, yet they're the same." Pay dirt. Omar's left eyelid lowered slightly. "There will be much to bond you and your friends soon. As you lay groundwork, others are finishing their constructions. When you are ready, so will they be."

With perfect composure, Omar asked, "And when would that be?"

As would any actor worth her Equity card, I read his face in a black hole of intuition. Omar knew, and I was too good at bullshitting not to be able to see.

"Two weeks, maximum."

I know this all sounds pretty darned swell, but I didn't have a clue as to what I was right about. For all I knew, it could be the con game to end all cons. It could be a plot to overthrow the government of Red China. I didn't know. But whatever the game, when Omar sat back in his chair, I knew it would begin within two weeks. Salim thanked me profusely and ushered the heavily robed woman into his spot at the table. I took the hint.

I told the Tunisian's wife that she was more important than she knew, and to persist in doing what she knew to be right.

I told the Tunisian's mistress of the evening that she was more important than she knew, and to start doing what she knew to be right.

I told Renchenkov that he should hook up with, say, Gorbachev's think tank, and work on his English for future speaking engagements.

Ivan hung back until sparkles of frustration-induced perspiration glittered on my face by the candlelight. He sat opposite and offered both his hands.

"I'd prefer a palm reading, if you can do that," Ivan asked.

Well, I certainly *used* to be able to do it. Annoyed for no real reason—frustration, no doubt—I dropped the happy-little-entertainer face and took his hands, one in each of mine.

BINGO. I was unblocked. Ivan might, indeed, be one hell of an economist; but he appeared out of nowhere into a place and at a time where all kinds of people were dropping like the stock market. Never looking down at the big man's palms, I started talking, never taking my eyes from his. Whatever I babbled, the eyes would give him away.

Running my fingers lightly down the center of both upturned palms, I said, "You are a complex man." Ivan's face smiled, but his gray eyes were locked, confident. Smug. "Subterfuge is so much a part of your nature," I lifted my chin, "that I'm not even sure you really want to take me to dinner. Perhaps you simply think you *should*." There was a minute flicker. Pay dirt.

"Oh. So you're saying I'm a liar." No animosity in the question. A probe. Another smile of the lips.

"I would if I didn't have a large vocabulary. I would say 'deceiver.' I would say your nonchalance is no more real than mine; just more refined—more serviceable, if you will. And the answer to your shared question is, within two weeks."

Ivan's eyes softened almost imperceptibly. Game and point. I won so he would stop playing. He leaned across the table on silent cue, and kissed my cheek.

Out of nowhere came my next questions.

"Is your mother Irish? Do you know where she is?"

Ivan's head tilted. A smile lit both mouth and eyes.

"No, and yes," he answered, tapping my nose as he left the table.

Then why did I have the strong feeling he would "find" her within a day or two? A false intuitive burp, perhaps, so I shrugged it off. And just about the time I thought I'd faked my way through to the Ivan payoff, David Wood sat down.

"I didn't expect to see you here," he said without a hint that it pleased him in any way at all.

Unconsciously, I sat slightly back in my chair. I tried to appear welcoming, all the while feeling guilty and uncomfortable for not having gotten back to him about dinner or a movie or whatever. Even a blocked person with the extrasensory perception of a potted fern could have felt David Wood's anger at me.

"Nor I you." I can't tell you how I hate it when someone is angry with me. I always want to run away, but my life had somehow become a series of locked doors. "Cut the cards, please, three times."

He did, and said without preamble, "You're not in the will."

"Mother insisted I be cut out years ago," I quipped, wanting this reading to be over more than a bad dental visit.

"Apparently so did my father. And apparently you didn't know that I drew up his final will myself a few weeks before he was murdered, did you?"

"Golly, no." What *was* he getting at? Those who know me well know that use of the word "golly" is the first clue that I'm getting annoyed with the turn of the conversation. "Gee" is another sure tip-off. "Gee, I guess I should have asked, huh?" I started laying out the cards. "Should I do a general reading, or do you have a specific question?"

"Only how you have the *chutzpah* to be in the same room with me after everything you've done. Let me tell you something," he lowered his voice, "if

Salim weren't making such a great offer for my
buildings, I'd spit on you. But I'll settle for making
you pay for my father's murder."

"I thought you believed in my innocence," I protested.

"That was before I saw how far you're willing to
go to get your hands on my father's property. There
isn't anyone you wouldn't fuck, is there?"

A truly lovely note upon which to end a grueling
session. I suspected his antipathy was more over my
not returning his telephone call than over any real
belief that I was carrying on with Omar so he would
buy me a not-very-attractive property on the only
street on the Upper West Side that had successfully
defied gentrification. I was, yes, speechless.

"I was admiring your window box while checking
out my new buildings this morning. Very nice."
Where was he going with my window box? "Your
friend Fran told me you were a botany major in college. That right?"

What had Fran done now? I couldn't think of a
reason to deny it, so I confirmed what young Wood
knew. "Yes. University of New Hampshire." I
wasn't about to admit to the year. I was in enough
distress.

"You have a green thumb. That's foxglove that did
so well outside your window, isn't it?"

Before I could, in my further confusion, agree that
the foxglove had done especially well this season, the
words caught. Foxglove. Digitalis. The flowers were

long gone and the leaves now brown on broken stalks, which—as any amateur gardener would know—does not in the slightest diminish their efficacy.

"The police were quite taken with your farming, Vic."

David left the table quietly, exuding gusts of disdain in his wake. I sat tired and stupefied, feeling as though the entire evening hadn't really happened. In my own defense, I *had* just gotten out of the slammer that morning. Ivan and Michelle brought me out of my daze.

"*Finis?*" Michelle asked.

"*Tout est bien qui finit bien,*" I mumbled hoping that, indeed, all's well that ends well. Not believing it. Knowing that an examination of the contents of Mr. Hillerman's stomach would reveal traces of dried foxglove.

Ivan placed a brandy snifter in my hand. "Michelle said I could grab a ride back uptown with you two. Hope that's all right with you, considering my reputation."

"What reputation is that?" Michelle asked pleasantly, having heard nothing, of course.

I threw about twelve dollars' worth of cognac down my throat in a shot. "Fine. You can carry me." I'd already been arraigned. Aside from the actual execution, the worst thing that could happen right away would be raising additional bail money.

"My pleasure." Ivan's arm went to my waist as I stood and Omar hustled to our side.

Handing me an envelope, Omar said, "Thank you so very much, Vic. My guests found you and Michelle absolutely delightful. Delightful," he repeated. "We still have a great deal of business to discuss, I'm afraid, but Ivan has agreed to escort you to your homes. You must be very tired after so much work." If he only knew how little, and yet how much. "My driver is waiting outside. And once again, please accept my heartfelt admiration." Kisses on both cheeks, and we were dismissed.

And I was finally, and completely, unblocked. Too late for the job, but intuitively regular again, nonetheless.

Back in the limo. Back uptown. Back across Central Park. I asked Ivan the question that had hit me during Salim's farewell, "No bullshit, Ivan. Are you a bodyguard? And if so, for Renchenkov or Omar? That's why you were at the Château d'Or tonight, isn't it? You're in some kind of business with both of them, and have been for years."

Michelle started laughing, then descended into overt giggles. Annoyed at her, I lit a cigarette. Annoyed with me, she rolled her window all the way down.

Ivan did not laugh at my query, but simply said, "You can search me if you like, but I'm not carrying a gun, Vic; I was just so damned glad to see you," which sent Michelle into paroxysms of new laughter for the remainder of our ride, all the way to my stoop.

Michelle never could hold her booze.

Ivan took my keys and led the way through the exterior door. He opened the apartment and handed me back my keys. "Thank you both for a most entertaining evening," he said, then shook his head in amusement. Suspiciously, I watched him chortling to himself until he was out of the building.

"Bodyguard?" Michelle sputtered as soon as we were inside.

"Well, I think it's pretty damned peculiar how many foreign nationals Ivan is tight with."

"I'd rather be tight with them than with some others I've been tight with," Michelle chuckled.

"I'm making you some coffee," I countered.

"I won't sleep."

"I don't care," I offered on my way to the kitchen. "As far as I can tell, you've had entirely too much fun this evening, as it is."

"Where's Slasher?" Michelle asked from the sofa.

"In your lap," I answered, proving my own point.

After two cups of Vienna roast, Michelle was better. In her resobered condition, she expressed the opinion that Ivan showed a great deal more potential than Sergeant Dan Duchinski in the long term. And, since he exhibited such marvelously amoral characteristics, was fifty times more likely to "wind my clock" in the short term.

That uncharacteristic euphemism earned Michelle another mandatory cup of coffee, but she had a point. Ivan had a definite free-from-guilt aura. In fact, he seemed rather free of everything.

For a man who had recently been dumped as an international banking executive, Ivan Stepanek seemed to be taking tending bar in, let's be honest, a less than four-star establishment pretty damned well. Cheerfully, in fact. Manners: impeccable. Dress: upscale. Education: dauntingly broad. Friends: impeccably upscale, and dauntingly broad.

Why would a man like that be so enthusiastic about a relatively short-term sublet of the Black Hole of Calcutta, complete with animal life? I questioned why a man like that would be in the slightest bit interested in a shallow broad like me?

Michelle couldn't figure it out, either. She and Slasher fell asleep diagonally across the bed, so I took the short sofa.

I thought it was an improvement over a holding cell cot. Of course, I also think that it's always darkest before the dawn. That, in turn, reminded me of grinding poverty and, so, the envelope Omar handed me at the end of the party. I opened it, and ten one-hundred-dollar bills illuminated my living room. Clearly, there was something that I didn't understand.

But as my dear almost-ex, Barry, always used to say when complaining about my tendency to overthink everything, "Always remember and never forget: a day without sunshine—is like night." Hard to believe, but that thought didn't clarify a lot.

I checked my watch. Midnight. The witching hour. Vic Bowering prime time. Jewel LaFleur comfort zone. The sound of Slasher's snores and Michelle's deep breathing wafted from the bedroom. I had the "screaming caffeine and life-crisis oodgies." and my available psychiatric health team was konked out. I considered the two Valium in the change section of my purse, found them powdered amongst the dimes and pennies, put on my shoes, and sneaked out the door.

JEWEL WAS DRINKING a Grolsch beer and watching Australian rules football again when I let myself into her apartment.

"Just a minute, darlin', Speedy Ian's about to squash Chuckie the Cutie. YES! YES!" Jewel turned the volume down a hair and pointed to the kitchen. "Get yourself a beer, sweetheart, and another for me, would you? The head bashing will be over in a couple of minutes."

I did as instructed, returning to slide into the little space left beside Jewel on the couch, and leaned against her as though I were three years old. She kissed the top of my head, said, "Woozy, woozy, woozy," and then, "KILL HIM, IAN!" When the televised carnage was complete and the score tallied, Jewel remote-controlled to pay-for-view boxing and hit the Mute button. "I expected you here for your woozies this afternoon," she said matter-of-factly.

"Then you heard," I mumbled into her soft shoulder.

"I hear everything, darlin'." Which was true. Despite her being housebound, Jewel's extensive network of fans and friends called and dropped by, night and day. I was living proof of that. Any New Yorker who can be consistently located is truly "a Jewel above all others."

"I didn't kill Mr. Hillerman, Daily, Lucy, or Wood, Jewel," I whined a little.

"I know that. Mr. Hillerman was older than the hills. And that poor Daily boy was in the final stages of AIDS. He'd been seriously depressed for a very long time. Personally, I'm not convinced that there has been even one murder committed, let alone four. No matter how many, you sure as hell didn't do it. Anyone with a brain would know that."

"The police don't. I have a window box full of a plant that produces the same poison that killed Mr. Hillerman. The funny part is that I planted it because it reminded me of my grandfather. I'm probably the only person in New York City with enough foxglove to knock off a city block."

"Yes, well, that is bad luck. What about Duchinski?"

"He's keeping an open mind, at least," I admitted, "but he doesn't know about my homegrown *pharmaceutica* yet. He's got Michelle baby-sitting me so that I have an alibi in case anything else happens." Jewel looked over my head as though searching for the invisible Michelle. "Oh," I explained, "Michelle had champagne *and* a cognac at dinner." I felt Jewel nod comprehension. "The joy-juice caught up with her. I came over because everything finally caught up with me."

"You're not missing Barry, are you?" Jewel asked.

I defended myself without admitting anything. "Well, he was always *there*. That was nice."

Jewel shifted her weight without making me move. "It was *not* nice, Vic, and he *wasn't* any more there then, than he is now." When Jewel's right, she's right, but a tear slid down my cheek anyway. "But I'm here for you, darlin'; I am always here for you."

I cried it out, while Jewel murmured rhythmically. "Woozy, woozy, everything's going to be all right; Jewel's here."

We sat like that for twenty minutes until I felt as though I could finally go home to sleep. I stood and said, "Thank you, Jewel. What would I do without you?"

"Probably end up in some loveless, sexless marriage to a man twice your age," she offered.

"The men twice my age are all dead now," I answered, feeling inexplicably bereft at the realization.

"There's always a silver lining!" Jewel smiled sagely. "Really, there is. It's not kind of me, I'm sure, but now that Lucy's dead, the neighbors don't have to muzzle their dogs. Mr. Hillerman and the Daily boy were suffering horribly. And with Wood gone, Barry has stayed my eviction indefinitely." Jewel looked directly into my eyes. "And, if they raise your bail, I have quite a nest egg set aside. You'll get most of it when I die, anyway."

"God, Jewel, not now."

"Just so you know, darlin'."

"Jewel," I asked, "I never asked before, but what exactly were Wood's grounds for eviction?"

Jewel laughed a satisfied rumble. "Oh, Ben Feldstein set my rent at one hundred dollars a month for the rest of my life before he sold the buildings. It was a condition of the sale. Wood argued that rent-stabilization made no provisions for that kind of rider and was bankrupting me with appeals to the board." Jewel noticed the crestfallen look on my sleepy face. "What is it, darlin'?"

"Just that everyone knows I'd do anything in the world to protect you, if I could."

"Oh, *that*," Jewel laughed again. "You are *not* going to be convicted of anything. I promise you." I must not have looked convinced. "I *promise* you, darlin'. Have I ever let you down?"

"Thanks, Jewel." I kissed her cheek. "I feel better." And I did.

Go figure.

Jack, Jack, and Jill (their real names being Jack, Jack, and Harold—which is another story, entirely), the three dancers who share one of the apartments in Jewel's building, were drinking white wine on the stoop. I turned down their offer to join them and let myself back into my apartment without incident.

Yeah. Sure.

SIXTEEN

Monday, October 29

WHEN I AWOKE on the sofa the next morning at ten-thirty, Slasher had managed to convince me in my sleep to draw my legs up around my chest to accommodate his body behind my knees. I came to consciousness in the same position as any adult corpse found in a small steamer trunk, and feeling a bit worse.

The minute I opened my eyes, Slasher yawned and walked sedately to his food dish. All he got for his trouble was a pack of semimoist. I hadn't slept very well.

Dreams of losing teeth, pursuit by malevolent strangers, and Barry Laskin do not make for a well-rested Vic Bowering. Michelle was still dead to the world. After my bath, she was still out of it. She hadn't roused, even after I had watched in perverse fascination "People's Court" (dog eats neighbor's cat), "Sally Jesse Raphael" (how child abuse causes cannibalism in adulthood), and "Nine Broadcast Plaza" (black and white people screaming at each other; Richard Bey profoundly asserting profound stuff over the din). When I started idly wondering whether or not anyone ever called the harried host

"Dick," in self-preservation I went against Duchinski's orders one more time and walked outside to sit on the stoop.

Mr. Feldstein was there when I arrived. He looked up at me from the bottom step where he was sitting and said, "Victoria, please join me," and swept a semiclean spot on the stair next to him with a liver-spotted hand. "How are you doing? I heard about your problems."

He looked so concerned, I couldn't bring myself to launch into my tale of woe. "I'm fine, Mr. Feldstein. Jewel said everything is going to be all right and, as you know, nobody disagrees with Jewel."

"This is true," he agreed. "This is very true," he agreed again and patted my hand. "Well," he continued, hauling himself upright with some difficulty, "I have a pressing appointment. Just needed to rest for a while. I think I'd better take a cab today."

"Would you like me to go with you to hail one?" I asked. Mr. Feldstein looked more frail than usual.

"No, thank you, sweetheart. I'm not dead yet." He kissed my cheek and pinched it.

"Mr. Feldstein—" I began, not certain how to say what I wanted to ask. It was a question that had festered during the night amid all the nightmarish periodontal and marital anxiety, and was suddenly clanging around where I didn't want it—in my conscious thought. "Do you think—" I paused and took a deep breath.

"What, sweetheart?"

"Do you think Jewel could have killed Wood and Loony Lucy to protect me, and maybe Mr. Hillerman and Daily to put them out of what she thought was their misery?"

There, it was out. Unlike a burp, it didn't make me feel a bit better.

"Oh, *bubchik*, is that why you look so tired this afternoon? Of course I don't think that our Jewel could do something like that. Of course not. The idea is—" he grinned, "—ridiculous. Ridiculous. Besides, what about the phone calls everyone has been getting? Even *I* got one. Saturday night, I remember, because I just cleaned out the Shabbes candlesticks. It was a man's voice, Victoria. A man. And, if you don't mind my saying so, there aren't two less manly women on the West Side than you and Jewel." He patted my hand again in amusement. "Now, you stop thinking like such a *meshuggeneh*."

"The cops think I can imitate a man's voice," I told him.

"Not in person, my darling. And I *know* your and Jewel's voices because they are like music to me."

"Exactly," I dourly agreed, kissing Mr. Feldstein affectionately for having tried—and failed—to comfort me and my nasty train of thought. I watched him hobble toward Broadway.

Any professional performer worth her character shoes ought to be able to alter her voice. And if ever there had been a consummate professional, it was Jewel LaFleur. She had stripped for Congressmen and kings, who had all firmly believed that she enjoyed it. If that's not acting ability, I don't know what is.

And unfortunately for my peace of mind, I *do* know.

I DASHED BACK into the apartment to hear the voice of Mike the stage manager angry over the tinny speaker of my answering machine.

"—tomorrow night and that's IT. Comprendo? Look, I put my two cents' worth in for you, Bowering, and you're making me look like an asshole. If you don't want blue gels on your lighting, get that contract to me TONIGHT. Not a threat. A promise. Your understudy is ready, willing, and eager."

Yeah, yeah. I've been threatened by men taller than Mike. Of course, they weren't *union*. Like Scarlett O'Hara I would think about that "tomorrow." At the moment I was on the way to wake Sleeping Beauty—and not with a kiss.

"MICHELLE!" I yelled, yanking the covers off her fully clad body. "MICHELLE, WAKE UP!" She grimaced up at me but didn't move. Slasher, intrigued by any activity whatsoever in my fallow bedroom, jumped up onto the sheets beside the—for all intents and purposes—paralyzed body of Michelle. "Michelle, get up, I have something to do and I need you along." Slasher meandered curiously across

Michelle's stomach and stared into her face. She stubbornly closed her eyes. Slasher bit her nose.

"Damn it, Slasher!" Michelle bolted upright. Slasher's usually benign right fang caught the side of Michelle's nostril, leaving a, well, for lack of a better word, slash. "Ouch." She rubbed her face. "What time is it, anyway?"

"Monday," I answered from the bathroom, where I had already turned on the shower. "Dunk yourself; I'll get you some coffee and antibacterial ointment for your nose."

There was a lot of grumbling, but Michelle did as she was told. She was probably intimidated by the puzzled look on the face of my attack cat.

After her shower and half cup of admittedly ancient coffee, I got Michelle into some of my clothes and out the door.

"Where are we going?" Michelle asked, stumbling a bit on the perilous surface of the sidewalk.

"To see Jewel," I answered. "There's something I have to ask her."

"Don't tell me. The telephone's broken."

"It's not something I can ask over the phone, Michelle." I hustled her up the stairs to Jewel's building, buzzed Jewel's apartment, and then let us in with my set of keys. "As a matter of fact, I'm not sure I can ask it in person. That's why I need you with me. I know you'll kill me if I chicken out after waking you up." I knocked my special code knock on the door and then fitted my key into the Medico.

"What couldn't you ask Jewel?" Michelle sniped. "The woman doesn't hide anything. Names, dates, places, all you have to do is ask and she'll tell."

I pushed the door open saying, "But you have to ask." Jewel was not in her usual place on the sofa. The television was turned off. "Boy, I hope we're not waking her up. Jewel always sleeps late."

"Oh, no. Is that sensitivity I hear regarding somebody's sleep?" Michelle demanded as she sat herself in a carved oak sidechair.

I ignored her. "Jewel, it's Vic and Michelle." I peeked through the hallway and saw Jewel's bedroom door open. To Michelle I said, "I guess she's in the shower. Let me make you another cup of coffee," and went to the kitchen. Just before I ran the water for the coffee, I listened to hear if Jewel was midrinse. Wood's new hot-water system turned personal hygiene into a confrontation with the Amityville Shower whenever another tap was opened. Hearing nothing, I ran a stream into the carafe. "I'm making coffee, Jewel, or would you prefer espresso?"

"Espresso for me," Michelle answered from the living room.

"JEWEL," I shouted, "do you want COFFEE or ESPRESSO?"

You have to understand that I've been a paid actor since God was a toddler, and when I project my voice, it can be heard in Winooski, Vermont.

"Could you keep it down, Vic," Michelle said
from the kitchen doorway. "I have a little head-
ache."

"Jewel!"

Michelle cringed as I raced past her toward the
back of Jewel's apartment. I had thought that my
nightmares were the pinnacle of the masochism of
my imagination, but I had no idea how quickly my
brain could process new, horrific scenarios, until that
moment in Jewel LaFleur's silent apartment.

I envisioned Jewel, fallen with a broken hip—or
worse, suffering a heart attack. I imagined finding
her, passed away in her sleep, in the oversized bed
with the souvenir pillows arranged around her silver
head. Then, like a club, my brain whacked me with
a vivid film of discovering the woman who had cradled me through every catastrophe New York City
has dealt me, lying murdered in the drapery dark-
ened gloom.

The bathroom door was ajar, but not entirely
open. I held the edge of the molding and reached my
left hand across my body to switch on the light.
"Jewel?" I asked, pushing the door open, my voice
bouncing off the ceramic tile. The hollow shower
enclosure seemed to echo the pounding of my heart.

"Vic!" Michelle's shout made me jump. She appeared behind me in the bathroom door. "She's not
here."

"What?"

"Jewel's not in the bedroom. She's not—oh, no!"

"No," I said, "Jewel's not here, either. She's not in the apartment."

"But that's impossible, Vic. She *has* to be here."

I lost my patience. "Jewel weighs about four hundred pounds, Michelle. She is not the sort of person who can hide under a bed or in a broom closet, now is she?"

"I don't believe it," Michelle muttered, rechecking the bedroom. "She's disappeared, Vic. Jewel hasn't been able to walk more than fifteen feet without hyperventilating in over ten years. Where could she have gone? Do you think she could have been taken to the hospital?"

"The stairs aren't wide enough for a gurney, Michelle. Remember when they took Mr. Hillerman's body to the funeral home? They had to grab ends of the body bag."

"I missed that."

"You were lucky. Besides, if Jewel had gone to the hospital I would have been notified. Jewel was either taken by force or lured out of here."

"Vic?" Michelle asked tentatively. "There is another way."

"What?"

"The shower is still wet, and there's a lot of water on the floor."

"So?"

"Jewel is too big now to get out of this building on a gurney."

"I *said* that. So?" If I didn't rely so much on Michelle's innate logic, I would have slapped her. Instead, in her own way, she slapped me.

"Too big to get out—in one piece."

I thudded heavily onto the toilet, staring into the dripping maw of the shower stall.

SEVENTEEN

Monday Evening, October 29

I MADE MICHELLE CALL the Twentieth Precinct to report Jewel's disappearance, figuring my credibility around there had probably plummeted somewhat during my last murder interrogation. Michelle used her very best "I am a rising advertising executive in New York City" tone, which was greeted with approximately the same amount of awe and fear that my "I am a struggling dilettante n'er-do-well" attitude gets me in any Manhattan bureaucracy: bored indifference. That forty-eight-hour waiting period you hear so much about on "America's Most Wanted" is no figment of a writer's fertile mind. The fact that Michelle was the fourth of Jewel's friends to have called made no difference.

After I'd received the seventh call asking me if I knew where Jewel was, I broke down and called Dan's beeper. He returned the call immediately from his desk downtown and insisted on speaking with Michelle. She hung up before I had my chance at him.

"You went out last night?" she asked me.

"I thought you were asleep."

"I *was* asleep. If I hadn't been asleep, you never would have gone out without me, and there wouldn't be all that new, swell incriminating testimony in your file."

"Now what did I do?"

"According to *three* witnesses, who know you personally, you were seen leaving Jewel LaFleur's building the night that she disappeared—making you either the last person to see Jewel alive or, conversely, just maybe the first one to see her dead." Michelle rubbed her temples miserably. "You know, Vic, you may be the dumbest person I have as a friend. No wonder you're still in the business."

"Oh, God."

"God had nothing to do with it. AND I don't want to hear a word about shitty karma. I don't want to hear a word at all. Dan's on his way uptown. Maybe he'll understand you, because I sure don't."

We rattled around in silence, punctuated only by my regular dialing of Jewel's telephone number—unanswered, for an agonizing two hours.

BLAHHHHHHHHHHHHHHHHHHHHT. The door buzzer drilled. Michelle peered through the peephole, said, "It's Dan," and let him in.

Without even looking in my direction, Dan told Michelle to go home, then went to the refrigerator and poured himself a large glass of milk.

"Dan?" I ventured.

"No," he answered. "Not yet. I can't listen to you," he exhaled loudly and picked up Slasher, "just

yet." Dan took a long pull of milk, and then tilted
the glass to let Slasher get a tongueful. When he had
drained the contents, he took the glass to the sink and
rinsed it carefully. After placing his service revolver
in the canned goods cabinet, the big man sat in the
puny Lincoln rocker, pushed himself forward and
back a few times, and said, "I give up. You've finally done it; you've worn me down. I'm man
enough to admit defeat."

"I'm sorry, Dan. Michelle was asleep, and I
couldn't stand being in the apartment another minute."

"Then I guess you're going to have one *hell* of a
time being in a cell for the rest of your natural life,
aren't you?"

"I didn't do anything, Dan," I said, moving to his
side and sitting on the carpet. He moved his arm
away from my extended hand. "Innocent people
don't get convicted of murder."

"And what goes 'round comes 'round; and good
will out; and he who laughs last, laughs best; and
peace on earth, good will toward man; and—oh, this
is a good one—the truth will never hurt you. I *give
up*. I don't know what else to do for you. The only
reason you're not in custody at this second is because I pulled in every chit owed me to guarantee I
wouldn't let you out of my sight." Dan watched the
ceiling fan rotate for a minute. "Have you talked to
Barry?"

That was a shock. In fact, it hadn't even occurred to me. "No," I admitted.

"No? Well, finally, I am truly surprised by your behavior. I'll admit, I expected to open the door and find him stuck to you like cat hair on black cashmere."

"Dan, what do you think happened to Jewel?" My voice was so steady, it frightened me.

"I think she's dead. We just can't figure out how."

I got up and walked to the end table, and picked up the telephone. In two motions, I hit the Auto button and the number seven. Dan got out of the rocking chair and over to my side.

"Who are you calling?" he asked.

"Jewel," I answered, my ear tight to the receiver. "I always call Jewel. She loves me. Jewel's always there. Always."

Dan depressed the disconnect, and took the phone from my hand. "We'll call tomorrow, Vic. It's late."

"Jewel doesn't mind, Dan. I need her now."

His hand covering mine on the earpiece, Dan said, "I'm right here, Vic. We'll try again in the morning. Right now, let's go to bed."

"I'm not sleepy."

"Yes, you are. And even if you're not, I'm more tired than I've ever been. Come to bed with me, Vic, and let me hold you. Would you do that for me?"

I sat on the bed as Dan rifled my dresser for nightclothes. He rejected several before handing me a white cotton lawn nightshirt I'd been saving for hotter weather. I stood and dropped my clothes to a heap on the floor, and pulled the ruffled vee over my head while Dan pushed Slasher to the bottom of the bed and pulled back the sheets. Duchinski pulled one of the fine pink satin ribbons at the neckline out of its entrapment inside the nightshirt, kissed me, and pushed me toward the bathroom. "Brush your teeth. I'll get the lights."

Most of the apartment was dark when I emerged from the bathroom, though a paler gray in the bedroom due to the security light mounted in the back alley. Dan was already in bed, wearing only his skivvies. For some reason, I was shocked. Not by the virtual nudity, but by Dan's underwear choice. I had always thought of the big cop as strictly white Fruit of the Loom. In retrospect, it seems odd—even to me—that colored bikini briefs would befuddle me so much under such normally provocative circumstances.

Slasher was sound asleep under Dan's left arm, so Duchinski lifted his right for me. I lay myself lengthwise against his side, my head on the knot of muscle near his neck, my right hand on his belly. The disgruntled cat jumped to the floor when Dan shifted to cover my hand with his. His right hand lifted the hair from the side of my neck, and stroked the hollow at the base of my skull.

"I can't lose her, Dan," I whispered into the curly black hairs of his chest.

"Shush, baby, shush. Don't think about it to-night."

"I just don't know what I'd do without her, Dan."

"I know, baby," he said quietly. "Believe me, baby, I know exactly how you feel."

EIGHTEEN

Tuesday Morning, October 30

I WOKE UP SWEATING. To be perfectly honest, it was probably the sweating that caused me to wake at all. Other than lying in damp sheets, I can't remember ever feeling more comfortable and secure. Still half asleep, I wiggled a bit to reposition for another several winks. My butt hit the proverbial immovable object: Dan Duchinski. No wonder I was sweating: my body temperature is not accustomed to accommodating the necessary adjustment made when sleeping with another human.

Dan's heavy arm pinned me to the bed at the waist. I wriggled some more to try and get him to roll over, but he was stuck to me like a burr. Slasher, hopeful at the signs of life from the bed, jumped up, threw himself on his back next to my face, and started his pigeon noises. From inside the back of my hair, I heard Dan mutter, "Morning, boy."

"Morning, boys," I responded groggily. "Dan, much as I'm enjoying the novelty of this Kodak moment, my bladder is singing to me." With effort, I lifted the hairy arm off myself and tried to connect with the real world.

Of course, the real world has never made it a point of waiting for me to connect with it. We're always on some sort of collision course, scheduled by the world and not me.

"Shit," I spat, swinging my legs over the side of the bed. "What time is it? Never mind." I grabbed the nine-dollar emergency phone off the windowsill by the bed and punched in seven numbers.

"Stop it, Vic," Dan commanded. But his center of gravity was off, and I stood out of his reach as the phone began to ring. "Don't do this to yourself, Vic. I'll—"

"Jewel?"

"Vic? For God's sake, what time is it?" Jewel's lovely voice came through my wonderful, hi-tech fiber-optic line. Dan regained his balance and grabbed the phone from my hand, putting it to his ear.

"Who is this?" he demanded into the mouthpiece. "Holy shit!" he said after a moment. "Stay right where you are; we'll be right over." There was a secondary pause before he hung up the phone with an explanatory, "Dan Duchinski. Now don't GO ANYWHERE."

"Jewel's alive!" I crowed to the ceiling.

"So it would appear," Dan confirmed—grudgingly, I thought. "Get dressed. We're going right over to talk to her. Shit. Where are my clothes?"

"I knew it," I shouted, ignoring him for the time being. "I told you," I rubbed it in. "I told you she was alive, didn't I?" With that I threw my legs around his lap, arms around his shoulders, and bit his neck.

"Stop it, Vic."

"Not yet." I said, refusing to let go. Not a man to be tied down to any woman, Dan stood up with me still attached to his middle. I crossed my ankles around his back, hanging from his stomach like a one-hundred-thirty-pound parasitic moss.

"Off, Victoria. NOW." I let go with my legs, but entangled my fingers in his hair. "You're not out of the woods, yet."

This was true, but after the gut-wrenching fear of losing Jewel, my problems seemed as minor an annoyance as being asked to belt a high C in a musical score. Blood was surging joyfully throughout my entire body.

Of *course* I kissed Dan Duchinski. Yes, there was a little rubbing, and a couple of those deep-in-the-throat noises, too. But I never forgot that I was raised properly.

"Dan?"

I think he said something like, "Nghhmm."

"Before we go over to Jewel's, could you please make love to me?"

Notice, I said "please."

Nevertheless, perhaps Dan was raised by wolves, because he twirled me about and pushed me to the rumpled bed.

And went to the bathroom.

I waited for him, naturally, but by the time he returned to the bedroom, any fool could tell I had lost my competitive edge.

"Get dressed, Vic. NOW." He took his own clothes to the living room. Dan was hanging up the phone by the time I was clothed and ready to leave. "I notified headquarters that Jewel has been located. Now, let's go, the gold shields will be meeting us there in an hour."

I guessed it was perfectly logical that the cops would have to look at Jewel personally. I mean, otherwise, any old murderer in the world could just call up the precinct and say, "Hey, never mind. The missing person's back! You can stop looking!"

Dan took Jewel's key out of my hand and took care of the illegal entry himself. I burst ahead of him at Jewel's apartment door, but my first look at her face stopped me in my tracks.

Jewel's snapping blue eyes were dull with fatigue; her normally vibrant peaches-and-cream complexion appeared vaguely sallow. Even her voice carried a hollow timbre.

"Vic, would you make some coffee? I'm too tired to get up."

"Jewel," I said, rushing to where she sat on the sofa, "are you all right? You look awful."

"Thank you, darlin', I'm fine. I told you, I'm tired, that's all. And, if you don't mind my telling you, you will look awful, too, when you're my age."

"Make the coffee, Vic," Dan instructed me. Then to Jewel he asked, "Would you mind telling me where you were last night, Ms. LaFleur?"

"Not at all, *Sergeant* Duchinski. Though I hope you will extend me the courtesy of asking you the same question," Jewel answered. I could almost hear Dan blush through the kitchen wall. I returned to the living room where I could watch it, upfront and in person, while the coffee brewed. "Vic, dear would you get me a glass of water, please. The stairs just about killed me."

I scurried out and back as quickly as possible and positioned myself next to Jewel on the sofa, soaking in my relief at having her next to me again.

Dan was intent, however. "Where were you last evening, Ms. LaFleur?"

Jewel checked her watch. "How do you know I wasn't here?"

"Because," Dan answered patiently, "Vic came over to visit you yesterday afternoon. When she found the apartment empty, she called the police to report you as a missing person." Jewel shot me a look of profound disappointment.

"Well, not only me," I defended myself foolishly. "Lots of your friends called in."

"I feel like a talk show," Jewel commented, once again looking at the time. "Vic, you'd better bring the coffee. This may take a while."

Now, I like being helpful, but my constant dismissal from the room was becoming frustrating. So, as I arranged the coffee service, I demanded, "You guys wait for me!" Which they did.

"Thank you, sweetheart," Jewel thanked me, and stirred two sugars into her bone-china cup. "Sergeant?" she inquired of Dan, who shook his head "no, thank you." I sipped out of my own special Jewel mug decorated with fornicating penguins. "I'll be happy to answer any of your questions. I believe I'm known for my openness," she smiled sweetly, "but first, may I ask why *you're* here, Sergeant?"

I thought I would be bored with Dan's answer, but I was double-whammy wrongo, once again.

"I'm here to arrest you for the murder of Harvey Wood, and Lucille Simmons. And perhaps a few others."

My coffee slopped in a tidal wave over the heads of giddy arctic birds, burning my mouth, and drooling down my T-shirt.

Jewel quickly handed me a tissue. "Are you all right, Vic?" she asked. I nodded numbly, and she turned her attention back to Dan. "I thought so, yes. Actually, I had hoped you would get around to me a little sooner. I'm sorry, Vic, dear. You should never have had to spend a minute in jail. I'll always feel guilty about that. Now," she said and sipped at her coffee, "what did you want to know, Sergeant?"

"Dan, please," the big cop requested, "like always."

"You started it," Jewel chided. "*Ms*. LaFleur, indeed."

"Sorry, Jewel," Dan started over while I sat, mouth hanging open, feeling slightly nauseous. "Now, where were you last night?"

"With my lover," Jewel answered smoothly. "Vic, would you hand me that tin of shortcake, please?" I was rooted by my ass to the sofa. "Vic? The cookies?" I uprooted and did as I was told. Jewel frowned at me. "Oh, for God's sake, Vic, don't look so surprised. Surely you didn't think I was a virgin when you met me." I shook my head no. Jewel put a shortcake cookie in my lap and closed the tin. "I've been meeting my lover the last Monday of every month for the last—" she checked her watch again, "—ten years or so. About the time we both started to get tired."

"Can your location be corroborated?" Dan asked.

"Certainly. It's not like we were sneaking around. Really!" Jewel looked offended by the very thought. "Just call the front desk at the Plaza. We have a standing reservation and I like to think I'm a difficult woman to forget."

"You are that," Dan agreed. I wanted to hate him for what he was doing, but the misery he felt shone through every pore of his skin. "Thank you for your honesty," he commended Jewel once more, "and now I have to ask you—"

Jewel patted Dan's arm and finished for him, "Am I a murderer?"

"No!" I blurted.

"Yes," affirmed Dan.

"No," Jewel answered placidly. "Not that I wouldn't have liked to bump off Wood. The idea simply never occurred to me. Naturally, I was doubly pissed-off when Victoria was wrongfully accused. Sometimes I wonder how the police can drive around the city handing out parking tickets, what with their heads stuck up their asses. No offense, Dan."

"None taken, Jewel." Dan lifted the all-but-forgotten cookie out of my lap and popped it into his mouth. "You know who *did* murder the victims, by any chance?"

"Victim. I know who killed Harvey Wood, the crud, may he ride through hell on a balloon bicycle with a flat tire." Jewel looked at the face of her watch one last time and asked Dan, "Do you have your car, darlin'? We can apprehend the perpetrator now." She handed Dan a piece of paper with an address written on it. "You can have your backup meet us there, though I can assure you that you won't need them." Jewel heaved herself upright, tapped my arm, and said, "Close your mouth, sweetheart. Don't want to catch flies."

Dan called headquarters and the three of us left the apartment together for the last time. As Dan was helping Jewel down the two flights of stairs, I ran back up to Jewel's apartment and let myself in. Opening the drawer in the Victorian Gothic side table, I located several massive rings of keys like the ones Carlotta always carried, grabbed them and streaked out and upstairs one more floor.

Dan and Jewel hadn't reached the vestibule before I trial-and-errored the correct key and opened the door to Loony Lucy's small studio apartment. I didn't even need to step inside to see what I was looking for.

The pieces all fell together in the jigsaw puzzle I'd been putting together in my mind.

I caught up with my cop and Jewel.

IT TOOK NO MORE than fifteen minutes to reach the conservative Riverside Drive address Dan had clasped in his hand. I sat scrunched in the back seat for the ride. Jewel sat like a queen in the front, her face rigid, as though it were carved of the finest marble.

"What were you doing upstairs, Vic?" Dan asked me, more weariness than aggravation in his voice.

"I got Jewel's keys and let myself into Lucy Simmons apartment."

"You must have found what you were looking for pretty quickly."

"Right away," I answered. "It was a lovely arrangement." I knew Dan would wait for the rest.

The doorman let us through with a respectful nod to Jewel. On the fifteenth floor, Jewel handed a set of keys over to Dan, and said, "No need to knock."

I could see Dan's reasonably suspicious cop mind start churning, and took his arm. I watched Jewel sadly, and told him, "It was Jewel's lover who murdered Harvey Wood."

"Of course," Jewel interjected haughtily. "I don't make it a practice to keep keys for every generic killer on the Upper West Side, you know."

"I know."

Dan opened the door, slamming it in its hinges out of old habit. As the uniformed police came up behind us, I finally caught sight of the man who had manipulated the electrocution of my landlord. He was sitting at his desk, in death as he had been in life: dignified and smiling slightly over a job well done.

I was going to miss Ben Feldstein very, very much.

Dan allowed Jewel to go to Mr. Feldstein and say her goodbyes without intervention. I suppose twenty years of police work lets a cop know when he's looking at a cut-and-dried suicide.

"What was it, babe?" he asked me of my trip to Lucy's apartment.

"A vase of ornamental weeds. Surprisingly well arranged."

"Of?"

"Several ornamental grasses, and a big clump of corn cockle."

"Poisonous."

"Definitely."

"Respiratory failure," Dan stated rather than ask.

"Asphyxiation. What she used on the pets."

"And?"

"A few stalks of foxglove."

Jewel patted Mr. Feldstein's hand, smiled regally, and strode toward us. She never looked back.

"Officer," Dan asked the lowest-ranking of white shields standing behind me, "would you please take the ladies home?" and he led the others into the sunny room.

EPILOGUE

Wednesday, October 31

ALL RIGHT, so after all the bitching and moaning, *kvetching* and complaining, I *could* have gotten the *Auntie Mame* contracts to the producers after Jewel and I left Mr. Feldstein's apartment. Jewel did everything in her power to get me to go away.

For the first time in my life, I didn't take her advice. But when Jewel told me she was perfectly all right and didn't need anyone to be with her, that was the first time she had ever lied to me.

I stayed over at her apartment that first night, listened to stories, poured champagne, listened some more, and threw my (ha, ha) career down the toilet. After everything we'd been through, I was far more certain of having another shot at a dipwah tour than I was of ever finding another friend like Jewel. So I stayed, and probably drove her a little batty, but she was stuck with me and knew it.

And I'm not sorry, either. So there.

Jewel did not shed a tear. I, of course, was a basket case over *her* loss. Well, mine, too.

Dan came and collected me the next morning. Frankly, I think Jewel was delighted to have her privacy back.

Duchinski and I sauntered into McAleer's in an effort to get back to our lives. Inexplicably, Kerry McAleer was behind the bar.

"Where's Ivan?" I asked.

"I had fantasies of him being with you," Kerry answered. "The big kielbasa never showed up for work. Called his place, whoever answered never heard of him. Never even picked up his pay." He shrugged as though such things happened every day. "Really needed another big guy around here last night, too."

"Trouble?" Duchinski asked without much enthusiasm.

"FBI, CIA, you name it. Every organization with an initial was here. Mary on a bike, who'd have figured?"

"What? What?" I repeated.

"Tommy Malloy, the quiet little teabag who sat at the end of the bar by the waitress station. Dragged him out of here like the bottom of a pond. Getcha a drink?"

"What?! Why?" I persisted.

"IRA," Dan shrugged. "And I don't mean a retirement fund. Malloy was running the Upper West Side Irish Republican Army pension and welfare fund out of here."

"Talk about inconsiderate," Kerry griped. "How 'bout a shandy?"

"No thanks, Kerry," Duchinski answered for us both.

Outside I accused Dan. "You weren't surprised about that raid at all, were you?"

"Of course I was."

"Liar." Dan took my arm and started walking. "What do you know, Dan? Who *is* Ivan Stepanek?" But I knew. Ivan wasn't really glad to see me that night he offered to be searched; he was packing. He didn't have an Irish mother as I accused when reading his palm, but Ireland was certainly being a mother to him. And as we all know, mother is only half a word.

"Let me guess," I prodded, "the arms were Soviet in origin, shipped through Middle Eastern channels, bought with American dollars."

"I don't know anything, Vic, and if I did, it would be classified. Now would you do me a favor and mind your *own* business long enough for me to get a promotion?"

We walked a block south to Seventy-ninth Street and Miss Elle's Homesick—a favorite of mine, especially when I'm not buying.

"So, I'm no longer under suspicion?" I asked from behind the tallest Pernod and water served in America.

"Absolutely," Dan said, hefting his beer, "but not for murder. As a matter of fact, as you guessed, your buddy Loony Lucy died of self-induced poisoning. Seems the chemical warfare she'd been waging against the animal kingdom went ballistic on her when she tried to improve her recipe by grinding the seeds in her Cuisinart. After the medical examiner managed to put aside your spectacular physical battery upon her person, it didn't take long to run the tests. Let that be a lesson to you.''

"Yes, sir. And could they match the varietal of foxglove in Lucy's pick-me-up bouquet to that in Hillerman's stomach?''

"Why do you ask me questions that you already know the answers to?''

"You're so cute when I piss you off.'' I grinned again. "Will we ever know if Wood had Mrs. Rivera and Tom Daily killed?''

"Daily was a suicide all right. As for Mrs. Rivera, we'll probably never know. At least we're sure Wood and Lucy won't go recidivist on us.''

"Ever the optimist.'' I ran my hand down Dan's thick forearm and took his hand.

He clutched nicely. "I suppose Jewel told you that Mr. Feldstein offed himself, too. He planned it with her and went on purpose, though.''

"I know. He was very sick.''

"I'll say,'' Dan said unkindly.

"Mr. Feldstein rigged that water heater to protect Jewel. He spent the better part of twenty years protecting her. He knew he was dying. Try and be understanding, Dan, it'll make you a better cop.''

"You really are nuts, you know that?''

"So I've been told.''

"How's Jewel taking it?'' Dan asked.

"She said she was happy that Mr. Feldstein went afterglowing."

"He would." Dan drained his glass and ordered another. "Jewel must have loved Feldstein very much to leave him, knowing he was going to kill himself. While I was sitting in her apartment, trying to nail her for Wood's murder, she was solid as a brick and counting down until her lover's overdose took. I think you should take a look at the kind of girl-friends you're hanging out with, Bowering."

"I have. Pretty neat, huh?" I smirked adorably. At least I tried. "I have a confession to make, though. Wanna hear? It's gooshily paranoid."

Dan kissed me with indulgence. "You thought Fran had killed everyone so she could get a better apartment, and set you up for the fall so she could bag your role in *Auntie Mame*."

So much for confessions. "Well, a case could have been made for it," I defended my instability.

"And you wonder why there's a male backlash. By the way, why don't you call Michelle and invite her to join us? God knows she deserves it for baby-sitting you."

"She's in Europe."

"Since yesterday?"

I raised my Pernod in Michelle's honor. "Omar cinched the deal with David Wood for the buildings and took Michelle to Vienna to help him celebrate. Seems he just came into some money." I gave Dan a conspiratorial glance, but didn't rub it in.

"I'll be damned."

"No doubt."

"I thought he'd have taken you."

"Oh, he asked." I looked over the rim of my glass into Dan's eyes. Jeez, how I love those eyes. Everything about Dan is so, for lack of a better word, "not actor." "I figured to get a better offer, what with it being my birthday and all."

Dan blushed like a Catholic schoolgirl, bless his hard little heart.

"Oh, by the way," he said, just as though he'd forgotten. "Happy birthday. Wanna rent a movie and order in Chinese?"

"Why, you sweet talker, what a fine idea," I answered, standing and leaving half of a perfectly good drink on the bar. "Let's blow this pop stand."

"All right," Dan grumped, throwing a twenty on the bar, "but this has been a rough week for me. I see that look in your eyes. Don't go thinking you can take advantage of me, just because I'm vulnerable."

"Who? Me?"

"All right then."

Dan is so cute when he's naive.

Everyone says so.

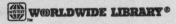

Live To Regret
Terence Faherty

An Owen Keane Mystery

First Time in Paperback

LOST...AND FOUND

Ex-seminarian turned sleuth Owen Keane has been hired to look into the strange behavior of his friend Harry Ohlman, whose wife, Mary, was tragically killed.

While observing Harry during his retreat in a small seashore town, Owen can't resist the allure of Diana Lord, an enigmatic beauty obsessed by a death that had occurred there many years before.

But as Owen gets closer to the truth about Harry, he is forced to confront his own feelings for Mary and his unsettled score with his friend—as crimes of the heart, past and present, unfold in Spring Lake and a town gives up its secrets.

Available in October at your favorite retail stores.

EMMA CHIZZIT AND THE MOTHER LODE MARAUDER

MARY BOWEN HALL
An Emma Chizzit Mystery

First Time in Paperback

DEATH PROSPECTS

Emma Chizzit, sixty-something owner of A-1
Salvage, is hired to help with plans to preserve the
historic gold mining town of Buckeye, California.

The savvy sleuth soon discovers that she's not
welcome, as rattlesnakes in picnic baskets and
threatening notes reveal. But the plucky Emma
is not fazed—until murder takes the spotlight.
She must expose dirty town secrets before a rush
of killing strikes the mother lode.

"Good mystery!" *—Rendezvous*

Available in September at your favorite retail stores.

WORLDWIDE LIBRARY®

EMMA

First Time in Paperback

A REID BENNETT MYSTERY

SOLDIERS ON THE SAME SIDE

An SOS from old Marine buddy Doug Ford brings Canadian police chief Reid Bennett across the border to the picturesque Vermont ski town of Chambers.

Ford, a local cop, is arrested for the murder of an attractive woman. Because he had not told anyone about the case he was investigating, no one except Reid believes he was framed.

As more murder paints the resort town bloodred, Reid uncovers a trail of dirty money that leads all the way to New York. He also realizes that the killer he's dealing with will stop at nothing to preserve his secret.

"Solid genre fare." —*Booklist*

Available in November at your favorite retail stores.

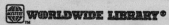 **WORLDWIDE LIBRARY**®

SNOWJOB

MURDER AT THE CLASS REUNION

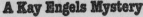

TRISS STEIN

A Kay Engels Mystery

First Time in Paperback

CLASS KILLER

After making it "big" as a New York journalist, Kay Engels returns to her twentieth high school reunion, hoping to find a good human interest story.

So when Terry Campbell, voted Best Looking in Her Class, is found strangled in her hotel bed while her classmates danced nearby, Kay's got her story. Terry had always been poison, and age had not impoved her.

As Kay puts her reporter's instincts into police business, she finds romance with the former class bad boy and uncovers a shocking secret in her own past. Then another murder brings her closer to a killer who will give her the story of a lifetime...but she may be too dead to write it.

Available in October at your favorite retail stores.

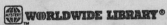 **WORLDWIDE LIBRARY®**

REUNION